Just in Time

for a

Highland
Christmas

A Highland Gardens Novella
Book 2.5

Dawn Marie Hamilton

ISBN: 978-0-9899642-6-5

This novel is dedicated to
those who cheer Christmas spirit.

ACKNOWLEDGMENTS

So many individuals helped bring this book to fruition, and I thank you.

Thank you to Cindy Davis for editorial guidance. To Cathy MacRae and Cate Parke for critiques. With a special thank you to Sarah Hoss. Words cannot convey how important you are to me.

Thank you to the members of Celtic Hearts, From the Heart, FF&P Romance Writers, and my Luckies for keeping me sane.

Most importantly, I thank Frank, my husband, best friend, and personal hero.

PROLOGUE

Fir-wood, Strathlachlan, Scotland, 1511

*T*hey weren't alone on the land. Branches rustled and cracked, the sound amplified by moist Highland air. Archibald signaled the men to silence.

A lone rider broke from an adjacent clump of trees, glanced around, then galloped through the amber grass, leaning low against the stallion's black neck. The slight figure looked over a shoulder once before darting into the wood at the far edge of the meadow and disappearing through autumnal foliage.

Archibald released a loud hiss. The path the fool had taken at risk to both horse and rider was nothing more than a narrow game trail, a dangerous track to approach at such speed.

"Ach, that ragged lad rides well," the redheaded Duncan exclaimed.

Archibald eased back in the saddle and threw his cousin a sideways glance. "He rides a fine piece of horseflesh, I grant you that. He is likely one of the Campbell's rash, young grandsons."

"Without guards, and on MacLachlan land? Nae Campbell

1

would dress in such tatters."

Duncan's aghast expression brought a smile along with a forgotten memory to Archibald. As green lads, he and his twin brother Patrick had dressed in servants' castoff garments and snuck away from Castle Lachlan for a jaunt in the Fir-wood. They later received a memorable scalping when Da caught them roaming about without escort.

"Must be a Campbell lad unaware of the border to our land. I am sure he will feel his father's disfavor across his backside before this day is through. That is, if he avoids breaking his neck first."

"Aye. For a fact, Chief." Duncan laughed. A hearty sound that never failed to cheer Archibald.

Poor lad. Duncan braved his temper on this frustrating journey. He'd owe the man a boon upon their return to Castle Lachlan after they fetched Archibald's bride.

"Let us be on our way, I want my lady ensconced within our keep before winter sets in."

He reined his horse to the left toward the more traveled trail through the Fir-wood, eager to reach Toward Keep, the stronghold of the Lamonts. Duncan rode at his side as captain while the rest of the *Lèine-chneas*, his hand chosen guard, followed a short distance behind.

The image of laughing violet eyes urged Archibald to a faster pace. He couldn't wait to hold the raven-haired Isobell in his arms again, inhale her intoxicating scent, caress her ivory skin, and kiss her pouty lips.

The sun set on the horizon. Crimson colors faded to mauve, a beautiful end to the day after its wet and trying start. Isobell Lamont spurred her horse to greater speed. She would escape the dictates of her overbearing father, even if she might die in so doing.

Her aunt in Glasgow would surely hide her, if Isobell avoided capture. Before she reached the burgh, however, she must cross the land of her unwanted MacLachlan betrothed, the hated Campbells, and other clans she didn't ken. She reveled in the knowledge her journey might be fraught with peril. She'd always dreamt of doing something truly adventurous.

The doing is never as grand as the dream. With a shake of the head, she ignored the nagging voice admonishing her and rode into the wind, the scent of fir in the air and an invigorating chill on her cheeks.

After risking discovery by crossing yet another open meadow, she eased the reins and sought the wood. Thank the good Lord the weather had cleared. She coaxed Dealanach Dubh into the shelter of a thick cluster of firs and slid from the stallion's massive back.

"Good lad," she crooned as she patted his sweaty flank, a horsy odor prickling her nose.

Isobell's stomach rumbled. *Should have raided the larder before running off in a rage.* Dealanach Dubh could graze on the sparse grasses, but what could she eat? Would she never learn to think before reacting to Da in anger?

She'd needed to escape, though, before Archibald MacLachlan arrived to fetch her. She wouldn't marry her clan's enemy even if she once thought herself in love with the man. It didn't matter that his once-beloved silver eyes, cleft chin, and chestnut hair still haunted her dreams, or that the thought of his warrior's body made her feel achy. She squeezed her eyes tight, refusing to shed a tear over a man who wasn't what she once believed him to be. *Grrrr.* And Da intended to force her hand. He'd signed the betrothal agreement with the blessing of the king, giving her no choice but to run away. What had changed Da's mind?

She jerked her eyes open and stared off into the wood. For the past year, he'd raged about the evils perpetrated by Archibald and his clan. She couldn't wed such a despicable man even if Da changed his mind and thought the match a good one. The men's plans would come to naught. She leaned against a large tree and smiled. Soon she would be in Glasgow, away from their schemes.

Wrapped within the false security of the dense trees, men's voices startled her. Everything within stilled. *What have I stumbled upon?*

After tying Dealanach Dubh to a branch, she crept closer to the voices, taking care to stay well hidden in the trees. In a wee clearing, a group of ratty men sat around a fire deep in discussion. She worried her bottom lip. Had she inadvertently stumbled into grave danger?

A sudden change in wind direction blew acrid wood smoke into her face. She sniffled, wrinkled her nose, and when she suppressed a sneeze, sagged against a tree in relief.

Gloaming was upon them, and Isobell strained to better see the men. Reprobates all. She started to scoot away— *Wait.* She recognized a few of them. Lamont warriors who'd left the clan in disgrace and, if rumors were true, taken up with Da's banished henchman Malcolm Maclay. The warriors must have joined this band of ruffians after Maclay died during a fight with one of Archibald's men.

She leaned forward to better hear the conversation. Perhaps glean something of import.

Most of their words were spoken in muttered whispers. With a frown, she edged closer, but then had second thoughts. Now would be a good time to leave before they learned of her presence. *Too late.* One man rose and paced toward her hiding place. Isobell fingered the dirk in her belt, ready to flee, but when he strode back to his cohorts, she held position.

"If we raid the MacLachlan encampment on the northeast border, we can make an escape across the disputed land with at least five head," the man spoke in a deep voice.

Humph. They were planning—

A large hand gripped her shoulder from behind and yanked her around. She froze, breath stuck in her throat, too shocked by the familiar face to pull free her blade.

"What have we here?"

CHAPTER ONE

One year later
Near the border of MacLachlan and Lamont lands

*V*oices raised in anger startled a foraging wren. The disparate normalcy within the scene of devastation struck Archibald in the chest, constricting muscle. Legs planted wide, he pounded a fist against his thigh. This had happened too often in the past year.

"Were all the cattle stolen?" he managed to ask through gritted teeth.

"Aye. I have failed you." The head herdsmen hung his head.

"Nae." Archibald squeezed the man's shoulder, offering solace. He couldn't allow the man to accept fault for *his* inability as clan chief to protect his people and livestock. Rage choked him, and he swallowed hard. "Fires still burn. They cannot have gotten far."

He grabbed his reins, anxious to give chase. The horse shied, rearing, sensing his agitation, yet the damn *brunaidh* remained steady where he stood on the beast's rump. Although a mere three feet tall, the MacLachlan clan brownie possessed oversized hands and feet. Feet that allowed for good balance.

Arms crossed over chest, muscles aquiver, Munn clenched a permanently wrinkled forehead even tighter and eyed the devastation from his superior position. The unusual blue-green of his eyes smoldered. Evidence of the wee man's ire caused Archibald's fury to flame hotter. This was the third raid in a fortnight. If they couldn't capture the thieves and recover the stolen cattle, the clan would be hard-pressed to survive winter.

"Lamont broke the truce," Archibald growled, heat flooding his face.

"You cannot be sure 'tis Lamont," Uncle Donald said. "Could have been Campbell men. Alexander threatened retribution. Should never have angered him by breaking his betrothal to your sister Elspeth."

One of the injured herdsmen limped forward and dipped his head in respect. "May I speak?"

Archibald nodded though his mind had shifted to strategy.

"There was something odd about one of the reivers—a slight lad who rode a fine beast with more skill than any man I have ever seen. A stallion the color of darkest night. And when the lad's cap slipped, ach, well, his long hair was like that of a lass and of the darkest night as well."

Archibald shot a glance at Duncan whose eyebrows rose in question. Could it be the same horse and rider they'd seen last year?

"See. I told you. The Campbell is behind this." Donald gloated. "Who else's lad rides such a beast?"

Archibald glared at his uncle. "We have nae feud with the Campbells so dinnae place blame where none belongs. Alexander's father is still the Earl of Argyll and holds command over the clan. He and I came to an accord; Elspeth's marriage to Finn was for the best. You agreed at the time." Archibald was sick to death of Donald's unwarranted hatred of their Campbell neighbors. For Christ's sake, his stepmother Mairi was born a Campbell, God rest her soul.

Hatred should be directed at the Lamonts. They were the ones responsible for Mairi and Da's disappearance and probable demise. Part of the never-ending feud. And the claims made by the addlebrained Finn MacIntyre were nonsense. People couldn't travel through time. His stepmother and father didn't travel on faerie dust to the future. They went missing after being chased by Lamont warriors, and certainly perished. If not dead, they would have found their way home before now. Archibald rubbed his chest where tightness threatened to crush him.

Damn Lamont and his clan. Damn them to hell.

Yet the description of the lad and horse resembled that of another lad who'd daringly crossed MacLachlan land a year ago. At the time, they'd thought him a Campbell, but he could have been anyone. No Campbell, to Archibald's knowledge, possessed dark hair.

Dark hair reminded him of Lamont's daughter Isobell, his betrothed, missing for the past year, and brought another dagger slice to an already-damaged heart. Their marriage had been meant to bring an end to the feud and peace to the neighboring clans.

"And you, Isobell, let me guess, you wish to wed Archie."

She nodded. "Aye. With all my heart."

Patrick and Isobell's words from so long ago haunted him, driving the breath from his lungs. What happened to harden her heart against him? Her father claimed she ran away so she wouldn't be required to wed. Why? They'd been in love. Why would she stay hidden? Could it be she wasn't in hiding— what if something had happened while she'd been out riding?

"Chief?" Duncan's voice startled Archibald.

He unclenched his fists and shook off the troubling memory. He would fulfill his vow to find her. Just as soon as he punished those who perpetrated the destruction that lay before him. Failure was unacceptable. The clan's survival depended on success.

"Aye?"

"Shall I stay and help?"

"Nae. You are needed for the hunt. Send a fast-running *gillie* to the keep to procure supplies and manpower to assist with the cleanup and rebuild—"

Munn's throat grinding made Archibald stiffen, certain he wouldn't care for the brownie's counsel. "Dinnae lecture, wee man."

"Said naught." Munn jumped from the horse and marched about the scorched land. "Nae Campbells." He sniffed the ground, glanced at the overcast sky, and scrunched his nose in distaste. "Nae Lamont warriors."

He paced, shaking his head and muttering.

Archibald banged a closed fist on his thigh in quick repetition. "Well? If 'tis not Campbells nor Lamonts, who?"

"Renegades."

"How do you ken such?"

"Just ken." Munn wrinkled his nose and sniffed again. "Ach, a female."

Archibald placed a hand over his mouth and coughed.

Duncan burst out laughing. "A woman traveling with reivers? You must be mad to think such, Munn."

The wee man bristled, rose to his full three feet, and glowered.

Archibald shook his head.

"Mark my words." Munn spun in a circle and vanished with the smoke from the smoldering fires.

Munn whirled onto the *Sithichean Sluaigh*, the knoll of the fae within the Fir-wood, spinning in tight circles, sucking leaves and other forest debris into the whirlwind surrounding him. Fuel for an all-consuming anger. When the rage petered out, he halted in front of Caitrina in a puff of smoke-infused dust.

The irritating *sithiche* coughed delicately and, with the flick of a slender wrist, the dust settled on the ground at her feet and dissolved. A wave of a graceful hand, and foliage poked through the velvety green grass, presenting vanilla scented phlox blossoms. *Showoff.*

She arched an auburn brow and tossed long flowing locks over a shoulder. "What do you want, wee man? Your summons interrupted important machinations."

"'Tis past time to make the third match."

Caitrina shrugged. "The queen refuses to reveal the couple's identities."

"I ken who they are." Munn jounced, hardly containing growing excitement.

Emerald eyes flared. "How would you ken the mind of the fae queen? *You* are naught but a wee brownie."

"Stop calling me wee." Munn glared at the halfling princess. "The queen requested my help once before."

"And you made a mess of things." Tall and willowy like most of her kind, Caitrina looked down her pert nose at him. He leaned forward, hands fisted.

"Did not."

"Did so."

Caitrina pressed a palm against his chest and pushed. He fell back a step, losing balance, but recovering quickly, glared at the faerie.

She had the gall to smile. "Well, if you are so knowledgeable, who are the pawns in the queen's game?"

Munn rocked back and forth, feeling smug. "Archibald and Isobell."

"Phew! Impossible."

"I smelled Isobell at the scene of a cattle raid on MacLachlan land."

"Did you tell your chief?"

"Nae. He does not believe what he cannot see."

"What does any of this have to do with the match?"

"Isobell must hate Archibald. When he learns she is not truly missing and has participated in the raids against the clan this past year, ach, he will never forgive her. A most impossible match as the queen's challenge dictates."

"Interesting. Perhaps—"

"Who else could it be?"

Caitrina raised a finger to her chin. "Not sure. Seems too easy for a final match. The last two matches traversed time, brought star-crossed strangers together. Archie and Isobell are in the same time and already in love."

"Were in love. I believe Isobell is mightily averse to a union with Archibald."

"Hmmm. There is that," Caitrina conceded.

"Then…"

"I sense something faulty with your logic. Oonagh has left the game board unattended."

"Where has the queen gone?"

"To seek out Finvarra in Ireland. You ken she wouldn't leave unless she believes she will win the final match. I can't allow her that success."

Munn understood Caitrina's concern. If the Queen of the Fae won the final match, Caitrina would never regain her royal status. She would remain a slave to the queen for eternity. As a halfling—half-mortal, half-fae—Caitrina would wither under the burden.

Munn shivered. He'd nearly faded into nonexistence at the whim of the queen when he failed to keep Caitrina from completing the first match.

The faerie's hands clenched and unclenched. "I cannot allow her to win. For Danu's sake, my father was a faerie prince. I should be treated as a prized princess. If only Oonagh wasn't so jealous of mortal women."

Munn smirked. "She would forget all else if she learned King Finvarra whored with a mortal woman again. You ken how flighty a full-fledged faerie is. The queen is the worst of all."

"There is some truth in that."

The King of the Fae was well known for his many trysts with beautiful mortal women. Something the queen found intolerable.

"So what about Isobell and Archie?"

"I am not convinced. Oonagh refused to disclose the target this time around. Why?"

"You think too much."

"Perhaps."

"So…"

Caitrina frowned, turned away, and then bestowed upon him a most *beauteous* smile. "Let the game proceed."

She vanished into mist.

Munn clapped hands in glee then spun in a circle and disappeared from the knoll too.

Isobell reined Dealanach Dubh to a halt, inhaled a deep breath to clear away the smell of smoke, and wiped soot from the side of her face. She hated the burning. Hated the useless destruction. But she hated Archibald MacLachlan more. So whatever it took to bring him and his clan to their knees…

"'Tis nae time to stop, lass. We need to keep moving."

Isobell threw a glare at her second in command. As always, his horrendous facial scars sickened her. Scars caused by Archibald's twin brother Patrick. Another reason to despise the MacLachlans.

She wiped soot onto already-filthy leggings. "We should split up here."

He sidled close, reining his horse in tight, and tugged on her loose hair. "Where is your cap?"

"Dinnae touch me." She slapped the dirty hand away.

"Aren't you still the high and mighty…" A mean look crossed his face and he worked his jaw before forcing a crooked smile. "Those raven locks of yours will be our defeat if anyone recognized you."

Her long hair had flown free of the cap when Dealanach Dubh took a jump too fast and they'd nearly fallen, but Isobell doubted anyone at the cattle raid noticed. She tugged the cowl of her tunic over her head. "The herdsmen were too busy fighting off our attack and putting out fires to notice my retreat."

"You better hope that is the case. If MacLachlan learns *you* are behind the raids, he will stop at nothing to capture you.

He will make you regret crossing him. Dinnae be thinking you can flash that comely smile of yours and all will be forgiven."

She smirked. "He has to find me first."

"Aye, that he does." Malcolm chuckled—his quick changes of temper sometimes made her dizzy—then glanced across the meadow to the game trail at the far side. "Dinnae like you going off unprotected."

"You ken I move faster alone."

"Aye. That does not mean I have to like it. Your father would never forgive me if anything regretful happened to you." As if that had mattered to Malcolm Maclay in the past. He hadn't held allegiance to her father in years, but the damage to his head from that fall from a cliff during a fight with Finn MacIntyre last year had changed the man, addled his senses. It had surprised Isobell and their band of Lamont renegades when Malcolm allowed her to take the lead of their small party of reivers.

Still, she didn't trust him. She slid a hand to her boot, comforted by the cold steel secured at her calf. And by the weight of the sword on her back.

Maclay caught the telltale movement and raised a brow.

Isobell inwardly cringed. It wasn't good to display any sign of weakness. She'd need to be more careful in the future. Maclay's health improved each day and, with his renewed vigor, he became more dictatorial. Soon he'd force her out, or worse. She mustn't let him get in the way of her revenge.

"We have been over this before. You and the lads take the cattle southeast to meet the traders and secure the funds. I will meet up with you on your return."

"Then be off with you." He slapped Dealanach Dubh's rump and the horse shot into motion, racing across the meadow.

Isobell hung low over the horse's neck, reveling in the speed. She would have her revenge.

After an uneventful trek across the disputed land, she slowed Dealanach Dubh to a walk as they approached the glade with its hidden cottage, cautious, senses alert. Something seemed off. Too quiet. She slipped from the horse and with reins in-hand crept closer.

Isobell covered her mouth to muffle a surprised gasp.

A beautiful woman, auburn hair spilling over narrow shoulders, sat on the hewn-wooden bench in front of Isobell's hideaway. A spotted fawn lay curled on her lap and two gray doves perched on an arm, like some woodland nymph. She shrugged and the birds flew away. Displeased with the motion, the fawn jerked to its feet and darted to the edge of the wood where a doe waited to greet it. Together they ran deeper into the trees.

"I ken you are there. You need not fear me." The woman gracefully rose and smoothed away nonexistent wrinkles from her green gown, the unusual iridescent cloth sparkling in the afternoon light. The green and purple *plaide* secured by an amethyst brooch at her shoulder displayed the characteristic pattern of a Campbell weaver, but Isobell had never seen the woman before.

Wary yet curious, she entered the small clearing within the shadow of the forest and faced the stranger. "Who are you?"

"I am known as Caitrina."

When the woman said no more, Isobell asked, "Why are you here?"

"To help you meet your destiny."

"What do you mean?"

"'Tis time to wed Archibald MacLachlan and bear an heir."

Isobell shivered and took a step back, jerked a glance from left to right, expecting Archibald to swoop in on horseback and whisk her away. No reason to panic. He wasn't there. When she returned attention to the woman, the woman was gone. Vanished. With a gasp, Isobell made the sign of the cross.

Who was the woman? A witch? A faerie harbinger of bad fortune?

There would be no wedding with the MacLachlan. How

could she wed with him after the sorrow he'd wrought upon her clan? Once upon a time, she'd thought herself in love with Archie. But then Da had told her of the despicable things Archibald had done to the clan and of the women with which he consorted and bedded.

Oh, why had Da forgiven him and signed the marriage contract?

Isobell glanced toward the woodland track. Quiet. Except for trilling birds and ginger-coated squirrels nibbling on pinecones.

Maybe she was mistaken. Maybe the mysterious woman merely strode away. Maybe the woman didn't ken of what she spoke. But a thorough search of the area proved fruitless, as did a search of the cottage. Isobell dropped onto the bench the fae woman had previously claimed. An unusual floral scent lingered in the air. Tears of despair prickled, and then fell unchecked.

What was she doing crying like a *bairn*? Enough! She swiped wet cheeks with a jerky motion. She was the daughter of a Highland chief. The strength of generations of Lamonts flowed within her blood. She refused to be trapped in an unwanted marriage.

Isobell leapt from the bench determined to flee before Archibald found the hideaway. From the cottage, she procured a chunk of moldy cheese and stale bannocks. After wrapping them within a cloth, she gathered warm clothing, placing the lot in a woven basket of heather, which was shrugged over stiff shoulders onto her back. Without a glance at the hovel, she straddled Dealanach Dubh and, with a heel kick, galloped from the only home she'd known for the last year—bent on escape.

CHAPTER TWO

*A*rchibald leaned forward in the saddle and eyed the approaching scout.

"The trail has disappeared as if it never existed," the lad confirmed his fear.

They had ridden the better part of three days and were nearly at the southeast border of MacLachlan land. How could a herd of Highland cattle, twenty head strong, disappear without a trace?

Wretched luck. Unusually dry weather followed by unending rain contributed to the feat surely. Glad the most recent storm had passed, Archibald shook rainwater from his wet hair like a dog. Would he ever get the smell of wet wool out of his nostrils?

Water gushed over rocks in the swollen burn. Gloaming would be upon them soon enough. Tonight they would sleep in the wet greenwood again. This wee glen as good a place as any. "Prepare camp. We will renew our pursuit at daybreak."

He scraped a tense hand over his face, bone weary. He could only imagine where the MacLachlan cattle would end their journey. Probably fattening some Lowland laird's larder.

Disgusted with the whole affair, he yanked the saddle from his horse. There was little talk over the fire that night, the men subdued. Their despondency was his fault. He'd never been meant to be chief. His eldest brother, Donald, thus named after their grandfather and sharing the same name with their uncle of questionable loyalty, was the firstborn and trained to lead. When he died too early, Archibald's twin, older by mere minutes, had been groomed to follow their father as heir. Archibald travelled on embassage to France for King James IV and lived a merry life until returning several years after Da and Mairi's disappearance and suspected demise—blamed on the Lamonts, of course—and became reacquainted with his twin's betrothed…

Isobell. The mere thought of her beauty left him breathless. Archibald adjusted his *plaide* and shifted his weight. The last thing he needed this night was an arousal.

He sighed and ran a hand through his unruly hair.

After Patrick's wedding to the outlander and subsequent move to France, Archibald became clan chief and inherited a future he never anticipated. The bright spot in his existence had been Isobell. He smiled. He couldn't help himself. They'd fallen in love.

Isobell had returned home, and he negotiated with her father, the Lamont, for a betrothal.

Archibald's smile faded. The memories were bittersweet.

Once the betrothal agreement was signed, he rode to Toward Keep to fetch Isobell. She'd put him off on several occasions while visiting relatives. Then she went missing.

Perhaps she hadn't changed her mind and run away. Maybe she'd disappeared as his parents had, never to be heard from again. Could the Lamont be responsible for his daughter's disappearance too? Archibald stared into the campfire, but the golden flames held no answers.

Duncan nudged him and passed a flask. *Uisge-beatha*—water of life. The whisky burned as it slid down his throat, spreading heat through his gut, fortification against the evening chill and his bleak thoughts.

Archibald woke before dawn, roused the men, and

resumed the search. Several fruitless days later, he admitted defeat and ordered the men back to Castle Lachlan and their families. He and Duncan searched for another day only to give up when they reached the border of the disputed lands. They could go no further without enraging their Campbell neighbors.

As they crested a ridge, Duncan pulled up short, raised a hand, palm outward, stopping Archibald, and pointed across the meadow below. Horse and rider burst from the tree line, racing straight for them. The same midnight stallion they'd seen before. Probably the same horseman. He noticed their presence, pulled back sharp on the reins, and halted the beast. The horse reared nearly tossing the lad who quickly regained control and altered direction, though lost speed in the process. Archibald slapped the rump of his horse and gave chase, Duncan and his mount on their heels.

Though horse and rider were light and fast, they seemed to tire quickly. Archibald felt the power of the horse beneath him and, with his thighs, coaxed greater speed from the animal. He and Duncan gained ground, each approaching from an opposite side, pinning the quarry between them. The rider flustered and the horse faltered, allowing Archibald to stay abreast and race for a distance until he was in position. Now! He leapt from his horse—a maneuver practiced often with his twin—and onto the back of the black stallion. Damn! A slight misjudgment sent him and the suspected cattle thief over the side, tumbling to the ground.

Grumpf! Archibald hit hard then lost his breath for the second time when the lad landed atop. He rolled quickly, taking control before the lad pulled a weapon. They had to roll again to avoid being trampled when Duncan's mount charged passed in pursuit of the runaway horses. Archibald maintained a firm grip on the lad's arms, avoiding thrashing legs.

The lad struggled, broke free, and crawled away, but Archibald tackled him back to the ground. With a quick move, he flipped him over, and pinned the lad beneath his weight. Then he froze. This was no lad. Soft breasts pressed against his chest and as the lass wiggled, his cock, cradled between her thighs, reacted to the friction.

What the—

He raised up onto his forearms, maintaining control, and quickly disarmed the lass of several blades. He slowly rose from her, and she scrambled to her feet. The cowl had slipped from her head, exposing long raven hair matching the cattle herder's description. Just who was this woman?

Archibald grabbed a fistful of thick hair and yanked it away from her face. Chin jutted forward, a familiar violet stare scorched him, and his gut ached as if punched.

He held his wayward bride-to-be—Isobell.

"Why?" The question torn from a tight throat.

"Because I hate you." Words filled with venom.

"Should have kenned 'twas you by the fancy gait of yonder horse." *And by his body's reaction to her pressed against him.*

"Dinnae hurt Dealanach Dubh!"

"What do you take me for? I would never harm such a fine beast."

"You only harm villagers?"

"What?"

"Swine!" She spit in his face.

He tightened the hold on her hair, hauled her closer, a breath away.

"Let me go." She squeezed his forearm.

He wanted to throttle her. Take her over a knee. Instead he shoved her toward Duncan and strode to his grazing horse. He couldn't come to terms with her hatred. Or her betrayal.

And what did she mean by *you only harm villagers?* He never...

"What do you want me to do with her?" Duncan asked.

Archibald held stiff, his back to them. He couldn't look at Isobell, the pain in his chest too great. "Take her on your horse. We ride to Castle Lachlan, where she will be sequestered in the pit until judgment is delivered."

Isobell gasped. "You dare not hold me in such a manner. I am the daughter of a Highland chief."

Archibald spun around and glared. "Do you ken how cattle thieves are punished in the Highlands?"

She blanched.

He hated her lean, disheveled appearance. Was obvious she wasn't getting enough to eat. But he must harden his heart. Offer no sympathy. His clan deserved justice.

They rode until nightfall, stopping to camp in a quiet glen. She hadn't uttered a word since her capture. It killed Archibald to tie her to a tree like a criminal. Unfortunately that was exactly who she was—a cattle thief.

Archibald motioned with his head for Duncan to step away to the fire with him out of Isobell's earshot. He placed an arm across the man's back, leaned close, and whispered, "Ride to Toward Keep. Meet with the Lamont. Request he reunite with his daughter at Castle Lachlan. I will escort Isobell to our keep."

Duncan glanced over his shoulder at Isobell. When his gaze returned to Archibald, deep grooves surrounded pursed lips. "I should not leave you without a guard. What if the other reivers learn you have her? They might attack."

"'Tis a risk I am willing to take. I want the Lamont at the castle to witness the wedding immediately upon our arrival."

Duncan hissed. "You plan to go through with the marriage?"

"I do. 'Tis the only way I can keep Isobell from suffering a fate worse than death."

"I dinnae like it, but I will do as you ask."

"Good lad." Archibald patted his back. "Be sure to inform the priest to be ready for our arrival."

After reallocating supplies, he watched Duncan ride away with Isobell's horse in tow then braced for a fight.

Isobell struggled against the leather strips binding her wrists until the raw skin burned and the pain near made her pass out. Bleary-eyed, she glowered at Archibald's back where he knelt by the fire. Fear made her stomach rumble. Or was it lack of food?

She couldn't remember the last time she'd eaten. And she couldn't guess when the next meal would be. 'Twas unlikely Archibald would offer anything beyond water if even that.

The rough bark of the tree dug into her back. Well, she'd better get used to being uncomfortable. Thoughts of what she'd cohabitate with in the MacLachlan pit made her squirm. And that would only be the beginning of the misery.

She stiffened at his approach, but noted the bowl he carried. Their gazes met. No emotion lived in the silver depths of his eyes. He placed the bowl on a nearby flat rock and just stared at her for a moment longer.

"Thought you might be hungry. I will release you to eat if you vow not to run."

Isobell cleared a parched throat, but only nodded, refusing to speak. What could she say? Deny her involvement in the raids? She wouldn't lie to him, but she would do whatever it took to escape.

Archibald frowned then bent and untied the binding.

Once free, she jumped to her feet and brushed the raw skin of her wrists with a light touch. What? Was that regret passing over Archie's fine features? As quickly gone.

His nearness made her stomach flutter. He still presented a fine form. Memories of better times bombarded her. She swallowed against the onslaught.

Remember—you hate him.

She scanned the area. Where was the best route to freedom?

He arched a brow. "Dinnae even think it."

She would never evade him nor was she fast enough to outrun him while he was awake. But once he slept...

She'd eat first. Not because it was what he wanted, but because it would provide renewed strength.

Isobell picked up the bowl and sat on the rock. He watched, arms crossed, eyes empty.

"Where are my cattle?" His rough-spoken words broke the silence.

She lowered the bowl from her lips. "I dinnae ken of what you speak."

"Isobell, this is not a game. You and your fine horse were spotted at the scene of a destructive raid. Men were injured. Cattle stolen."

"You surely have many enemies, among whom it is certain at least one exists who wishes to inflict revenge upon your person and clan."

"Is that what this is about? You believe I have done something to deserve your desire for revenge?"

"Aye."

He shook his head. "My clan will demand justice. The punishment will not end with a mere flogging."

"And what of my clan and the atrocities perpetrated against it by you and yours?" Archibald knocked the bowl away, grabbed her arm, and pulled her up. His grip was hurtful. She glared. "Let go of me."

He pulled her against his chest. "Where are my cattle? Tell me."

His breath was hot on her face. She felt the entire length of him, muscles coiled with rage, through the thin fabric of the lad's rags she wore. So different than when she'd longed for his touch over a year ago, wearing garments of many layers, dressed as a woman.

They were both breathing hard. The silver of his eyes went molten with lust.

So he still wanted her. Something to use against him. If she could distract him, perhaps she could filch one of the blades hidden on his person. She leaned in and rubbed against his burgeoning arousal with invitation.

He inhaled a gusty breath before laying siege to her mouth. The kiss was not as expected. She whimpered and drew his tongue into the moist recesses of her mouth. It had been so long since—

She chose to ignore the insect that buzzed past her ear.

Archie shoved her to the ground. She hit hard with a thump, hurting her hip. He landed on top and covered her mouth with a hand.

"Whist," he whispered. "Your fellow thieves just tried to put an arrow into you. Why, I wonder?"

More likely they intended to pierce his heart and she got in the way. The telltale sound of men moving through underbrush gave her hope for escape from the fate Archibald planned for her. She squirmed, trying to break free of his grasp.

"Keep still, you fool," he growled in a quiet tone. "Dinnae move until I tell you 'tis safe." Archibald crept away. Moments later, the sound of blade striking blade rent the air.

Isobell refused to remain put and wait for Archibald to haul her off to Castle Lachlan to stand trial. She jumped up, waved arms in the air, and hollered, "Over here!"

An arrow shot past, narrowly missing its mark—*her*.

She dropped to the ground and scooted behind the tree to which she'd previously been tied. Archie was right. They were after her. Why?

Arrows whipped past the tree in frightening numbers. The clang of steel became maddening since darkness had fallen and it wasn't clear if Archie was winning. She hoped he would. She didn't want to die this night.

The moon cleared a cloud, shedding light onto the clearing. A man screamed and fell. Another—one of the men she previously led—replaced him. By some miracle the flying arrows kept missing the fighting men. As an arrow landed in a nearby bush, she made a dash for Archie's horse and grabbed her sword from the scabbard attached to the saddle where he'd stowed it earlier.

She hesitated, unsure what to do. An arrow winged past. Her chances of surviving this night might be best served with Archie.

She jumped into the fray positioned at his back. Thrusting and parrying, arm growing heavy, she at last yanked the blooded sword from the dead man at her feet. The one

Archie fought soon lost his head.

Her blade slipped from a trembling hand and landed next to the gruesome sight. Archie grabbed the sword, swiped it over the dead man's tunic to remove most of the blood, and replaced it in the scabbard along with his claymore.

Isobell slipped to the ground onto her bum, curled forward, and sucked in large quantities of air, hoping the nausea would pass.

"Do you plan on telling me why your band of renegades is set on killing you?" Archie dropped to sit beside her with a grunt.

It could be only one thing—Maclay didn't want anyone to ken he survived the fall from the cliff. *'Tis probably in my best interest to keep that wee secret to myself. For now.* She shrugged. "Dinnae ken."

Archie pursed his lips, looked at her hard, and released a loud sigh. "Come on, we need to be away from here before the others return with more arrows. He tossed her onto the horse and leapt up behind. Too close for comfort.

"What do you plan to do with me?" Her voice sounded as tired as she felt, but she'd had to ask so she could prepare for the worst.

He didn't answer, just kept riding. She held stiff, leaning forward away from his body, so not to be affected by his manly assets. She couldn't allow fond memories to soften her feelings toward him. Naught had changed between them. Escape remained essential, and she now had two factions to avoid.

After she'd given up on learning Archibald's intent, he said, "Perhaps 'tis time for a truce."

CHAPTER THREE

Archibald smiled. Isobell hadn't held the stiff position for long and, as they rode, gradually leaned back against his chest, succumbed to exhaustion, and fell asleep. Soft strands of raven hair teased his cheek. The lass was a mystery. Being close, remembering the kiss, made him hard and needy. They'd been so in love once upon a time. Lips thinned, he shook off the raw emotion.

After they reached Castle Lachlan and wed, he'd need to learn the reason for her disloyalty and ensure no opportunities provided for future betrayals. He'd put a son in her belly quickly, God willing. That should keep her busy and out of trouble.

Unable to stop, he slid inquisitive fingers over the curve of her face. Much changed over the past year—matured. Violet eyes fluttered open and she smiled, until realizing she draped his lap. Isobell bolted upright, putting symbolic distance between them.

He shouldn't hang onto the hope of their love returning. With a sigh, he guided the horse out of the trees and across the moor above Loch Fyne. The weather had changed. A breeze off the water brought a chill, and he wished the lass wore warmer garments.

The sight of Castle Lachlan on its islet in the bay filled Archibald with pride. It always had. Each time he returned home.

"Snow." Isobell sounded surprised. The first flakes of the season floated to the ground and quickly melted.

"Aye. Aine claims to have read the signs. We should expect an early winter."

Aine MacTamhais had taken care of the household at Castle Lachlan for as long as Archibald could remember. What would she think of him wedding Isobell once she learned the lass participated in the most recent raid?

Perhaps neither Aine nor the rest of the clan needed to learn of the lass's participation. Duncan would keep the secret if asked. No one else needed to ken the particulars.

If only he could convince Isobell to keep their battle private behind the closed door of the bedchamber. The thought of wrestling with her on the big bed in the chief's bedchamber brought a half-smile and an image of other things they'd do together on that same bed.

The images shattered when realty arrived along with the lad running from the stable to offer assistance. Archibald threw him the reins, leapt from the horse, and then reached for Isobell.

"I hate you."

Her declaration was a clear reminder of the battle awaiting him. He lifted Isobell from the horse and purposefully slid her rigid form down his front. Let her feel the demands of his body.

He wasn't expecting the slap across the face, the sound overloud, though he should have. The stable lad's eyes rounded, and he drew a blade. Another lad approached, dirk in hand, ready to defend his chief.

A shake of the head signaled them to stand down. At the same time, Archibald grabbed Isobell's wrists to stop any further assault. The lads seemed unsure, but finally gathered he had things under control and went back to their tasks. "The next time you lay a hand on me in anger, I will put you over a knee and spank you until you beg forgiveness."

Jaw tight, she tugged her arm free, which he allowed.

"I ken. You hate me," he said when she opened her mouth to retort. She shut it with a snap. Their reunion was going poorly, but he supposed it would be too much to expect more under the circumstances. "I also ken you will agree to all my demands, from this day forward."

Her brow furrowed. "What are you talking about?"

"I plan to protect you from your foolishness."

The brazen lass had the nerve to snort.

"Come." He took hold of her upper arm and guided, half-dragged, her down the slope to the beach where a *currach* waited. "Get in."

Isobell scowled, but did as asked. The wee boat, made of skins and wicker, rocked, more so when he climbed in behind. He rowed in silence.

He wanted to ask questions. Learn what role she played in the raid. Had she been involved in other raids? Who was their leader? Where were the cattle? Instead he held his peace, perhaps afraid of the answers.

Was he daft to go ahead with the wedding? Did he risk his life? Time would tell.

When they reached the opposite shore, he sprang from the boat and dragged it onto the shingle. He took hold of her arm to help her from the craft, but she pulled free. "Dinnae need your assistance."

"Ach, but you do."

He reached for her, but she hopped out and kicked him in the shins. Before he thought better of it, he tackled her, rolling so he took the brunt of the fall, then rolling again to pin her beneath his weight. "You need discipline."

She squirmed. Bucked. Tried to push him off, without avail.

He held her prone. Hated treating her roughly, but she fought him at every step. What had happened to the Isobell he'd fallen in love with so long ago? Did she still exist?

"You bastard," she spit, eyes taking on the hues of a

stormy night.

"And you have a dirty mouth." Of which he felt the need to possess.

Fraught with emotions held in check for far too long, Archibald seized and conquered. Isobell yielded with a whimper then responded in kind.

When the kiss ended, they both panted. He found it hard to look at her eyes. Nor did she seem willing to look at him.

The sound of a clearing throat and then a chuckle was a splash of cold water to Archibald. What was he doing rolling on the cold, wet ground with his reluctant betrothed?

He jumped up quickly and helped Isobell to stand.

She averted her gaze, but not before he saw moisture glistening on her lashes. He banged a closed fist against his thigh then glanced at his grinning uncle.

Archibald had the urge to shed some of the tension coiling his muscles by punching Donald in the face. He swallowed the impulse. "What news, uncle?"

"I see you and Isobell have come to an accord. And not too soon. Her father awaits with the priest in the council chamber."

Isobell held trembling fingers to tingling lips. She was a fool. She'd thought to use Archibald's physical desire against him. Instead, he'd used his lips to easily bring her into submission. 'Twould be in her best interest not to allow him to kiss her in the future.

His kisses were too sweet by far. And why was he so free with them if he believed her a criminal? Her father claimed Archibald bedded many women. Sometimes taking multiple partners. A rogue. He'd even take a woman he deplored.

He wouldn't dare touch her in that manner again. Certainly not. She refused to be added to the number of conquests.

Isobell held her head high and allowed the men to escort her into the castle. Shocked gasps sounded through the great hall as she entered. She half-smiled. No doubt she looked much different than from her last visit. And not only due to the tatters she now wore, but because she'd changed much while trying to survive during the past year on the fringe of civilization.

She scanned the chamber, looking for Da. The great hall was much the same as she remembered. Dim light ventured in through the leaded glass of the high windows. A man lingering near one of the many tall, iron stands, face illuminated by candlelight, resembled her father. But no, 'twas one of her clansmen, proof the Lamont abided nearby.

Her roaming gaze landed on the large hearth and the roaring fire. She shivered, wishing Archibald would seat her in one of the several cushioned chairs near its warmth. He wouldn't. Not with the way she was dressed in filthy rags. She might ruin the green velvet.

Nor would he trust her away from his side. Not that she blamed him. With the first opportunity given, she would escape the castle and hide from not only Archibald but also Maclay and the Lamont renegades.

"This way." Archibald directed her in the opposite direction toward the stairwell.

Before she took a step, a plump older woman hurried across the stone floor toward them. Aine? Isobell remembered the gray-haired woman being kind during the last visit to Castle Lachlan.

"Tsk, tsk. You must be chilled to the bone, lass. Come with me. I have a comfortable chamber waiting with a warm fire and hot food." A gentle arm wrapped around Isobell, and Aine whisked her away from the men. "Your father has brought several fine gowns."

"Wait!" The demand stopped them mid-step.

Archibald strode to their side, and clutched Isobell's arm. She feared pulling away, his anger palpable. Aine peered at him through narrowed eyes.

"My lady needs meet with her father and the priest first then she may prepare for…" He let the words trail off.

Isobell gulped, more than able to fill in the rest. To prepare for her trial and judgment. And a priest? To give last rites? Could Archibald plan to condemn her to death?

He'd implied he would protect her. To what length? At what price?

When she joined the reivers, she'd been aware death might be her fate. Yet she'd never believed she would be captured, concentrating only on the act of revenge.

The silver of Archibald's eyes had turned to ice. He grasped her elbow, and she let him guide her up the circular stairs to the next floor.

A substantial space, the council chamber revealed the prestige of Clan MacLachlan, from the well-polished oak flooring, to the elaborate wooden screen with slats weaved in complicated Celtic knots, to the gem-laden goblets in the aumbry. Had she wedded with Archibald last year, she would have added to the wealth.

Her father and a man dressed in the frock of the Blackfriars of Glasgow strode toward them with purpose.

"My dearest, Isobell, you will not mind if I dinnae embrace you in your current..." With a frown, Da swept a hand indicating the garments she wore. "MacLachlan, why wasn't she given a bath and fresh garments before presentation?"

"I want the contract signed now. Afterward, she can bathe and return for the festivities."

"What contract?" Isobell glanced from man to man. "What are you talking about?"

The priest leaned in close. "You must consider your limited options. Under the circumstances, 'twill be in your best interest to sign, my dear."

Archibald frowned, brow furrowed. "I gather Duncan shared how we found Isobell?"

Her father nodded solemnly then pulled her aside. "You were always a difficult child. I spoiled you, but nae more. Marriage will be better than the, um, alternative."

Marriage? She turned on Archibald. His impassive gaze

bore into her. "I will not wed with you. No one can force me to say vows."

Archibald glared at his betrothed unable to understand why Isobell would rather go through with a grueling trial and risk a dreadful punishment than wed. "You must."

"Says you?"

"You wanted this marriage at one time." He towered over her, hoping to intimidate.

"Aye. As a young foolish lass hurting from Patrick's callous rejection."

"Would you rather have wed my twin?" Archibald hated how much that thought hurt.

"Nae!" Isobell looked horrified. At least there was that.

"Donald? Had my eldest brother not died?"

Isobell shot a nasty look at her father. "Da has been determined to wed me to a MacLachlan chief since my birth. How tragic. I have had three betrothals, to three brothers, and none suit."

"We suit just fine. You were once more than happy to agree to wed with me. Had you not, I would have returned you to your father after Patrick's wedding to Lady Laurie, and found another woman to bear my sons."

"Well, I dinnae want to wed you now. If you try to force me, I will see to it you have nae sons."

The priest gasped. The Lamont's face reddened. Archibald felt the effect from her statement as intended, a sharp pain in the center of his chest, but he couldn't allow the hurtful words to sway him. "You will change your mind."

"Nae!"

"Then shall we have a trial and sentencing instead of a marriage? I will spare nae leniency."

"As you see fit." Her challenging gaze never left his.

"Fine. Secure the prisoner." He signaled the men standing guard at the doorway to take her away. They'd been instructed earlier if need be to lock her up in a storage cell in the basement. He refused to order her thrown in the pit. He just couldn't inflict that indignity upon her. He hoped a few hours imprisoned would bring her to her senses.

"MacLachlan, you cannot." Her father stepped forward.

"I can and will." He nodded to his lads.

She allowed the men to usher her from the chamber, head held high. Her sense of pride matched his. At any other time he would appreciate it. Not now.

Archibald prayed she quickly reconsidered her choice. Before others learned of her crimes. Only as his wife could he keep her safe.

CHAPTER FOUR

*M*unn entered the council chamber and grinned. Maids and *gillies* hurried to and fro, making ready for the wedding feast that would take place after the pledging of vows. He was sure the chief was up to the task of bedding the lass and planting his seed. The third match would be complete. Caitrina would be free to return to *Tir-nan-Og*—the fae land o' heart's desire—and the MacLachlan clan would be blessed.

He was certain the lass would come around and pledge her troth to Archibald along with her love. If she continued to refuse, Caitrina would do something to make the lass change her mind.

Lines furrowed his forehead as his skin started to itch. Caitrina's unusual fae scent, a combination of peony, freesia, and sandalwood perfumed the air before she shimmered into corporal form in front of him.

"You were wrong," she said without preamble.

"Dinnae tease."

"Oonagh returned from the sojourn in Ireland and provided the players for the last match."

"Archibald and Isobell," Munn said. "Admit I was right."

"Cannot."

He frowned. "Then who?"

"Nae concern of yours." Caitrina faded.

"Wait! You must help with Archibald and Isobell."

"Not my problem." And she was gone. Vanished to another time and place.

Damn Caitrina. Munn huffed. What was he to do? Archibald and Isobell needed to be matched. 'Twas their destiny.

Munn crossed arms over his chest and scowled. Why was the lass resisting? Archibald was a man with a full head of hair and numerous teeth. Did she think she could do better?

Bah! The chief should drop her into the pit to linger for a long while. At least until she cowered like a proper wife. Munn scratched his chin and scoffed. None of the other wives he kenned were submissive to their men. The Highlanders grew weak. Led around by lasses in skirts.

He shook his head. 'Twas a damn shame.

Ach, he needed to think. Invisible to the others in the hall, he paced from the chief's table to the aumbry, one end of the council chamber to the other and back, and again.

An argument near the hearth rumbled in the background. Archibald and the Lamont disagreeing yet again on how to handle Isobell's rebellious ways. Another stubborn lass came to mind—Lady Laurie.

Try the wine. Spontaneous inspiration came over Munn. Why hadn't he thought of it sooner? He spun in a circle and travelled to another part of the castle.

❀ ❀ ❀

Isobell pushed against the heavy oak panel again. When it wouldn't budge, she kicked it. Pain shot up her leg. She grabbed the offended foot and hopped back, crumpling onto a pile of grain sacks. Damn Archibald MacLachlan.

She wrapped arms over her chest in a self-hug. How long would they leave her in this dark place? Would she give in if they left her long enough?

Boots sounded on stone. She tensed. Someone with a heavy foot approached her prison. Perhaps she'd learn her fate soon. The waiting drove her mad.

The door flew open and slammed against the wall, making her jerk. She shielded her eyes against the bright light coming from the torch Archibald held.

"Is it time?" she asked, stomach churning.

"Are you ready to sign the marriage document?"

"Nae."

"Then tell me the names of your accomplices. The ones who tried to kill you in the wood."

"Just some men I met in the forest."

He exhaled a gusty breath. "And, as strangers, they invited a lone woman to join their merry band of thieves instead of deflowering her?"

She inwardly cringed, but shrugged for Archibald's benefit. He could ask as often as he wanted, but she would never reveal the lad's identities.

"Isobell, tell me who else was involved in the raid."

She remained silent.

"For all that is holy, Isobell, they tried to kill you."

He was right. Her men had turned against her. Maclay probably commanding it. He didn't want his secret revealed. Still she wouldn't give them up.

"Fine. Agree to marry me and I will forget your part in the raid."

"You will never forget."

He sighed heavily. "I will return shortly, I expect you to sign the contract."

Left in darkness again, Isobell quelled the desire to have a good cry. A scratching noise, probably a rat, made her jump. Still, this cell was better than the pit.

An unnatural light suddenly illuminated the cell. A wee man with a bewhiskered brown face, a mere three feet tall, spun in a circle, stopping in the center of the small chamber. Isobell blinked several times in surprise. The man grasped the waist of the baggy brown leather *trews* he wore and yanked them up while puffing out his chest as men often are wont to do, then wiped his big hands on a fine woolen *leine*.

"And you are?" Isobell smiled, forgetting the moment of fright, guessing the identity of the man by the large crystal brooch holding a *brat* in place around his shoulders.

"My name is Munn." Unusual blue-green eyes sparkled. He swept the funny looking, pointed, green cap from his head, displaying pointed ears, and bowed with a flourish. "Have you never heard of me?"

"Aye. You are the MacLachlan clan brownie."

"True enough. Brought something for you to drink." He handed over a goblet of wine.

"Why?"

"'Tis wrong of the chief to lock you away down here in the dark bowels of the keep without food or drink."

She eyed the wine, and then the man with suspicion. Why would Archibald's wee man offer her kindness?

"Does something trouble you, lass?" Munn asked.

"Nae." She inhaled the fruity bouquet, took a sip, and smiled.

The wine was delicious. The best she'd ever tasted. She sipped a wee bit more, and then some more. Warmth spread through her, making her feel achy and needy. Where was Archie when she wanted him?

Archibald paced from the hearth in his study to the writing table and back. Isobell's father sat in one of the chairs before the fire, the priest in another. Neither seemed concerned over Isobell's reticence. Both imbibed in a taste of Archibald's finest claret.

"Ease be with you, lad." Lamont chuckled. "She will come to her senses."

Archibald glowered at the man and continued pacing. Moments later, he was relieved to be disturbed by a knock at the door. When he opened the oak panel, he found one of the guards from the cellar shifting weight from one leg to the other, staring anywhere but at him.

"What is it?" Archibald demanded.

"The lass."

"Aye?"

"Ach, well…" He tilted his head and frowned. "She's singing."

"Aye?"

"Merrily."

"Singing? Merrily?"

"Aye, Chief."

What could the lass be about? Archibald brushed past the guard, took the stairs two at a time, uncaring his shoulders scraped against rough stone, down to the basement and to the storage cell where Isobell remained confined. He hoped.

Sure enough, she was singing. *Merrily.* A ribald song about a couple of drunken warriors and a tavern wench. Loud enough to be heard through the heavy, roughhewn door. What else had the lass learned during her sojourn as a thief? He grabbed a torch from one of the guards, edged open the door, and peered in.

Isobell swayed from side to side with the melody of the song, one of the goblets from the council chamber held loose in one hand. She leapt into his arms and hugged him tight, goblet dangling from her fingers. "Archie, I have missed you so verra much."

"Have you, lass?" He raised an eyebrow, chuckled, wary. What was she up to?

"When is the wedding?" she demanded.

Fearing he might burn the armful of woman clinging to him, he handed the torch to a guard whose round-eyed look almost made Archibald laugh aloud.

"Are you drunk, lass?"

"Nae. Just happy we are finally together."

"What made you change your mind?" he asked in a soft voice as if dealing with a timid foal. He held her at arm's length, trying to discover if she played him for a fool.

Isobell wrinkled her brow in a most comely way. He wanted to kiss her, but first needed to understand what provoked the drastic change of heart.

"Why do you ask such a silly question? I have not changed my mind."

"Earlier, you refused to wed with me."

"You must be mistaken. 'Twas Patrick I dinnae wish to wed. I have always wanted to be your wife." Her smile melted all the ice within Archibald's chest, but still...

Uncertainty plagued him.

Did the why of it matter? Not really. The important thing was she was more than willing to say the vows. It would be in his best interest to bring her in front of the priest before she changed her mind yet again.

CHAPTER FIVE

*I*sobell inhaled the scent of lavender and appreciated its tranquil effect. She luxuriated in a hot bath afore a glowing fire in Archie's bedchamber. Soon to be her bedchamber too. She felt the smile on her lips all the way to her toes. She reached toward the nearby table where her goblet sat, but couldn't quite reach.

"Here, let me get that for you." Aine spread the silver wedding gown over the furs on the mattress of the big bed with its deep blue velvet curtains and scurried to the table then handed Isobell the wine. "Dinnae drink too much, though a wee bit will ease your nerves."

"Thank you, you are too kind."

Aine smiled, then made busy with preparations.

Isobell never thought to wear silver to her wedding, but the embroidered gown belonged to Archie's stepmother Mairi. Aine claimed he'd be pleased to see her wear the dress. Besides the color would look lovely with the blood-red rubies he promised as a wedding gift. She was the luckiest woman in Scotland. Tonight was her night.

And Archie's evening too, of course.

She glanced at the bed, supposing she should be nervous about the bedding. A thrill ran through her. Archie would be gentle.

"Ready, lass? You dinnae want your skin to wrinkle." Aine assisted her from the tub, and with a chambermaid, fussed over patting her dry with large cloths. They dropped a soft chemise over her head and sat her in a chair to let the heat from the fire dry her long hair.

Isobell sipped carefully from the goblet Archie's wee man gave her so not to spill. Delicious. She'd need to ask Archie where he procured such a fine vintage. They should put some aside for when Jamie visited. The king would be much impressed.

The maid braided Isobell's hair, threading silky ribbons of silver and red through the ebony locks, creating a lovely coiffure. Donning the satin gown, she shivered. Not from unease but excitement.

She stepped to one of the windows on the courtyard side of the chamber. Torches in sconces on the outside walls illuminated the falling snow. Much heavier than earlier in the day.

Where had that thought come from? Isobell frowned. She didn't recall seeing snow earlier in the day. With the effort to remember, her head started throbbing.

"Are you all right?" Aine placed a hand on her sleeve with the gentlest of touches.

The woman's honest concern eased Isobell; she turned away from the window and all troubling thoughts. "I am fine."

"Well, all young brides are nervous." Aine's smile was genuine, so different than the servants at Da's keep.

Another twinge of pain, but she breathed through the discomfort and decided 'twould be best not to think too much.

A manly knock at the door made her stomach flutter. Though only for a moment.

She took one last sip from the goblet, placed it on the mantel, and hurried across the chamber, stopping when Aine raised a hand, then slowed the pace to a more demure walk, ready to greet her future husband and all it entailed.

"Ready?" he asked when she greeted him.

More ready than he need ken.

He struck a fine-looking figure in his saffron *leine* and *plaide* of red and green. Archibald rubbed both hands down the length or the wool as if uncertain of her answer.

"Aye." She reached up to run a finger through a curl of his chestnut hair. Silver eyes flared and a lovely smile curved his lips. The cleft in his chin all the more obvious.

"You look lovely, dearling." He clasped her fingers, brought them to his lips, and feathered a tender kiss over them. "Shall we?"

She wondered at his arched eyebrow. Did he worry she'd refuse?

"Of course," she said.

Archibald placed her hand on his arm and together they approached the circular stair. He descended first, providing a barrier against a fall in the event she slipped.

Down two flights, and into the family chapel where her mouth dropped open in awe. Candles bathed the chamber in radiance. Golden light leapt and flickered, causing shadows to dance upon the walls. Rich incense drew her forward. Da and the priest waited at the altar.

Faerie wings fluttered in her belly as she crossed the chamber, Archie at her side. She would soon be his wife.

"You have made the right decision, Isobell." Her father slid sheaths of parchment across the altar.

Archibald placed an inked quill in her hand. She held the quill poised over the wedding contract and glanced up. All three men stared expectantly.

Archibald watched Isobell with something akin to fear. Would she sign? Or was her changed behavior a ploy of sorts?

She scratched the point over the parchment and finished the signature with a curly embellishment. Archibald released a breath and added his name to the document, dripped wax upon the page, and applied his seal. Isobell's father did the same, as did the priest.

Thank the good Lord, the deed was done. All that remained were the vows.

Archibald inclined his head toward the guard at the door. Shortly thereafter, family and closest retainers entered and circled the bride and groom to witness the ceremony.

The priest bade them kneel. Archibald assisted Isobell then dropped beside her. She gazed at him with a look of such love that amazement stole his breath.

Her actions made little sense. He wouldn't complain though. She was giving him what he wanted. *Be careful of what you desire. You may receive more than anticipated.* His father's warning from childhood flashed through his mind, and he swallowed uneasily.

Archibald startled when the priest cleared his throat. "Are you ready?"

An abrupt nod to the priest, and the man began reading from a prayer book, though Archibald barely heard the words, too obsessed with morose thoughts. He said the proper responses when bade and listened to Isobell recite her vows.

Relief washed over him and he gave into the urge to lift Isobell and swing her in a circle when the priest named them chief and lady-wife. He gently set her on her feet and kissed her soundly.

Those in attendance whooped and hollered. Several moments later, he and Isobell entered the council chamber to cheers, the clan welcoming their new mistress.

Thankfully, they didn't ken her sins.

With a palm cradling her back, Archibald escorted Isobell through the throng of clansmen to the high table. He didn't want to fall under her spell because of the circumstances that brought them to this day, but her lavender scent—a gift he'd given her—was intoxicating. He leaned close to her neck and inhaled the womanly fragrance.

She laughed softly, and he kissed exposed skin.

A hoot rose from the crowd.

Several others joined them on the dais, the Lamont seated to his right. The man leaned in close. "You best hurry and get her bedded and breeding."

Archibald tightened his fist but fought an urge to punch his new father-in-law in the face. He might be at odds with Isobell, but the man had no right to be crude at her wedding. Rather than create an uproar Archibald let the slight pass.

Musicians entered, set up on a raised platform, and tuned their instruments.

Isobell patted his leg. "We are expected to partake of the first dance."

They rose and performed a ring dance with others from both clans. Moving away, and then returning to Isobell, Archibald marveled at her display of genuine happiness. She laughed and joked and swirled with the other dancers as if having nae care in the world. As if, just days before, she hadn't participated in a cattle raid against him. And spit in his face. *Absurd.*

She seemed to have forgotten everything that happened over the last year. It was as if they had stepped back in time to when they first fell in love. A chill snaked over his spine.

He didn't like thinking of time travel.

The remainder of the evening became a blur of celebration. Before the crowd became too raucous from drink, Archibald swirled Isobell across the oak flooring toward the steps to the upper level so he could whisk her away to their bedchamber unnoticed. He hoped to bolt the door before revelers joined them to witness the official consummation of their marriage.

He preferred that moment be private.

He captured her hand and she giggled as they climbed the dim circular stairs. The music and revelry faded. Without stopping, they raced to the bedchamber and fell, laughing, into chairs afore the fire.

Then they both quieted. The moment Archibald had waited for so long was finally upon them. Would she be a willing mate or had she been playing a role this night?

She coyly gazed from beneath ebony lasses and moistened her lips. His cock jerked in response as if she controlled the thing with a string.

Would he ever forgive her part—though he believed it trivial—in the raid?

He cleared his throat. "Let us not harbor thoughts of troubling events from our past, even if only for this night." He clasped her hand and held it over his heart.

She tilted her head to the side and her brow wrinkled, as if trying to understand. Then her lips curved into a smile filled with, could he hope, love. "If that is your wish, then 'tis my desire also."

He nodded. From the pouch at his belt, he withdrew a leather wrapped package. He dropped to a knee in front of Isobell and presented the wedding gift.

Her eyes misted as he placed the treasure into her trembling hand. She opened the package to reveal the ruby ring, with its large gemstone, he'd had made for her, years ago, when he prayed she'd someday become his bride.

Isobell smiled though showed little excitement. She'd kenned of the ring from the beginning. "Thank you, husband."

He'd had other gifts made too. Ones she didn't ken about. With the tenuous circumstances surrounding their marriage, he'd keep those locked away until—

Better to think pleasant thoughts tonight.

"Would you care for some wine?" he asked.

"Nae." Her gaze landed on the bed then returned to him. "I would prefer to remember this night with a clear head. But first…" From a pocket sewn into a seam of the wedding gown materialized a small packet, which Isobell handed over with a shy smile. "I also have a gift for you, *husband.*"

He liked the way her voice emphasized the word. Perhaps they could make their marriage work. Accepting the gift, he carefully removed the wrapping. His eyes widened when a large ruby dropped into his lap. He stared at it for a might too long, swallowed hard, and then looked at Isobell.

She blessed him with a radiant smile.

"Thank you," he said, at a loss for other words.

"'Tis for the cross section of your claymore."

"Aye, I will be the envy of every warrior."

"And the target of many a thief."

Her nonchalant comment sobered Archibald. He'd added a new layer of complexity to his already-complicated life by marrying a woman who might possibly want to do him harm.

He sighed, stood, and reached out a hand. He led her to the bed where he undid the ties of her gown, allowing it to pool at her feet. The translucent chemise brought attention to the fullness of her breasts. She quickly covered them with trembling hands, hiding the desired bounty.

A chill slithered over Archibald's skin along with a foul thought—had she been with another man or, worse, raped?

"Are you afraid of me?" he asked.

"Oh, nae." She shook her head adamantly.

Relief near made him giddy. He raised her chin with a finger. "Look into my eyes. Trust me."

She complied, and he held her gaze while removing the hands that concealed the delectable feast from which he wished to partake and spread her arms to the side and clasped her hands. With an ache of yearning long harbored, he leaned in and sucked first one pebbled nipple through the cloth, then the other.

Isobell whimpered and swayed. "Ah, Archie?"

His heart jerked with pleasure. It was the first time she called him by his nickname since her capture. With as gentle a touch as he could muster, he slid the chemise over her head and eased her to the mattress where he dined on her bounty to the loveliest sounds a woman could make—moans of pleasure.

When the first waves of passion passed, Archibald removed his *plaide* and *leine*. Isobell watched his every move, a small smile gracing her moist lips. His cock jerked, and he rushed to rejoin her on the bed, more than glad the long wait was almost over. Raised on forearms, leaning over her, he studied her face. Rosy cheeks from the scratch of his whiskers, an impertinent nose, expressive violet eyes softened from their loving, and ebony eyebrows arched in question.

"You ken there may be discomfort?"

She answered with a hasty nod.

He stroked a finger along her soft cheek, along the front of her neck, and over a firm breast to linger on a pert nipple. She sucked in a sharp breath and arched her back, encouraging him to continue exploring. He splayed both hands on her flat belly, moved one between her legs, and teased her to a fevered pitch. When fragrant cream coated his fingers, he eased between her thighs and, edging within the slick folds, entered heaven. She stilled. "Easy, Lass."

"I am fine. More than fine."

The fit was tight. He moved slowly, hoping to only inflict minimal pain. As their bodies adjusted, she moved with him. Slow and gentle. When he hit the barrier of her maidenhead—thank the good Lord she was still a virgin—he thrust.

He captured her scream with an open-mouthed kiss.

His orgasm shot him to the stars. Pleasure so intense, he yelled Isobell's name.

She yawned and promptly fell asleep. A slight stab of inadequacy furrowed his brow. He'd make it better for her next time.

Archibald rose from the marriage bed, tiptoed to the hearth, and banked the fire. He removed a goblet from the mantel. Some wine remained. He downed a good portion then gagged. Bitter. The remainder he tossed into the fire. He stumbled and the goblet slipped from his weakened hand to the floor.

Whew… He wobbled. Something was amiss. Was the wine tainted? He shot a glare at Isobell, her features innocently composed in slumber. Had she meant to poison him?

He stumbled to the side of the bed and collapsed. Panted

through a wave of nausea. Clambered atop the mattress with effort. Worked his way to Isobell, hovered over her, and found enough strength to shake her awake.

Her eyes jerked open, big and round, and full of fear.

"You have poisoned me." Vision blurring, he plunged forward and passed out.

CHAPTER SIX

*I*sobell jolted full awake. Archibald's dead weight half-sprawled over her torso. She could hardly breathe. What had happened to him?

You have poisoned me.

What had she done? Memories returned in an unending wave. All the terrible things of which Da accused Archibald. Stealing cattle. Burning villages. Killing men. Raping women.

In horror, she shoved at him and tried to push him off. He barely budged. She reached back, grabbed the bedpost with both hands, and struggled to pull free. Finally, she dragged the last stuck foot from under his weight.

Scrambling off the bed, she grabbed the discarded chemise from the floor. As she donned the garment, she noted the blood on the inside of her thighs. *Grrrr.* A glance at the bed confirmed the proof of the consummated marriage. She'd never be free of Archibald, now.

She rushed to the table where a bowl and pitcher sat waiting. A vigorous scrub with a wet cloth and the evidence on her person was gone. The soiled sheet was another matter. She crept to the bed. Archibald snored like a drunken warrior. She tugged on the sheet, but couldn't free it from his weight.

Damn! When he woke, he'd find the proof.

Isobell frantically twirled the ruby ring on her finger, the color of blood, like the blood on the sheet. She wanted to deny its significance. How had she gotten herself wed to the vile man? How had she ended up in his bed? No longer a virgin, and wishing to forget the deed.

She needed to leave. Now. A crumpled silver gown lay on the floor. That would be of no use. She kicked it out of the way and searched for her lad's clothes, hoping they hadn't been destroyed.

Thank goodness for busy servants. Laundry had been left in a basket near the hearth, her tattered garments included. The lad's natty boots lay nearby. She quickly dressed and rubbed soot onto her face. Pulling the cowl over her head, she tiptoed to the door and listened.

Only muted voices coming from the on-going celebration below. Good.

She needed weapons. Not wanting to waste time, Isobell grabbed Archibald's claymore. Too heavy. Ah, but there in a dark corner, her sword leaned against the wall.

She'd prefer to also have a dirk, or two, or three, but had no idea where Archibald stashed his blades, and didn't have time to search. She needed to be gone before he woke.

He grunted, flailed an arm, and inhaled a gusty breath. She spared a moment to pause at the bedside table, where a piece of leather cradled the large ruby she'd gifted to Archibald. Removing the ring from her finger, she switched it for the gemstone, which she shoved into a hidden pocket sewn within her *trews*.

The sale of the gem would provide needed funds.

She snatched Archibald's *plaide* from the floor, and made quick work of draping it like a man. Hopefully, she'd be mistaken as a visiting clansmen.

Another listen at the door, and she eased the carved panel open. No one to the left. No one to the right. She skulked along the corridor, praying she wouldn't be recognized by the servants scurrying to attend the guests.

Instead of exiting through the great hall, she took the circular stairs to the kitchen, skirted the large prep table, and lunged for the door. The staff was too busy to pay any mind. Hand on latch, she took a bracing breath, and shoved the heavy wood panel open. Wind whipped her face. Ankle-deep snow covered the courtyard. She clung to the shadows, hugging the castle wall, dragging her feet to make the footprints look less like that of a woman.

Once clear of the yard, she ran to the beach and, with a grunt, dragged a *currach* across the shingle and shoved it into the icy water. The current tried to steal the boat, but she was too stubborn to let go. On the opposite shore a beacon light burned in the stable. She climbed aboard and rowed across the bay, struggling to keep the small boat on course.

Luck was with her; the stable lads snored in the hay. They'd be telling the truth when they claimed not to have seen her. She fitted Dealanach Dubh with a saddle, hoisted onto his back, and departed the village without waylay.

The heavy snow would cover their tracks, but made the going difficult. She followed a trail seldom used through the Fir-wood, wanting distance between her and her new husband.

Cursed life. She was wed to the evil MacLachlan.

He believed she tried to poison him. Though he hadn't planned to hang her for reiving, he'd certainly see her swinging from a gibbet for attempted murder no matter the charge false.

She held no illusions, he'd search for her with unwavering determination. Her only chance was to ride for Glasgow and procure passage to France. Distant relatives lived there who might agree to harbor a fugitive.

The going was easier out of the wind, within the protection of fir trees, but she needed to guide Dealanach Dubh carefully, away from tree wells, into which he might sink and break a leg or worse. They emerged from the trees into a clearing. The blizzard had worsened.

They rode until she realized they crossed their own tracks.

They'd ridden in circles and were miserably lost. Leaning forward in the saddle, she shielded her eyes, unsure which direction to travel. In the distance, a bright white light beckoned. Dealanach Dubh trudged toward the glow.

Archibald's wool *plaide* pulled over her head gave minimal protection as they slogged through the blinding snow, the light guiding them to who kenned where. Isobell clung to Dealanach Dubh with fingers numb from cold. Icy flakes stung the exposed skin of her face. Yet they followed the light taking them further from Castle Lachlan and the man who would never forgive her for an act she didn't commit.

As the storm worsened, Isobell wondered if she'd gone mad, risking life itself, traipsing over a countryside experiencing the worst weather of the season. For what? To escape a man she once loved. Was it worth killing her horse and possibly losing her life over such?

Should she go back and plead her case? If only she could curl into a ball and fall asleep in the snow and forget. Feeling drowsy, she started to slip, but caught herself before falling.

Isobell. Isobell. Fear not.

What? Who said that? She raised her head and tried to see through the blowing snow. The white light remained; drew them ever closer.

Emerging from the trees, they stepped out of the snow onto a mound of the most unusual green grass. Grass that should be autumn-brown. Above, a full moon shone bright. How was that possible? Isobell jerked a look over a shoulder at where they'd just been and gasped. The blizzard raged. Falling snow created a heavy curtain of white.

She patted Dealanach Dubh's ice-crusted coat. "Where are we, lad?"

A place of magic.

"'Tis known as the *Sithichean Sluaigh*, a faerie knoll." A golden-haired woman of inconceivable beauty sat a stunning white horse. "Dinnae fear this place."

Isobell arched her back, stiffening in shock, and inadvertently kicked Dealanach Dubh, who reared on hind legs. "Easy lad."

She couldn't bring him under control. He nervously skittered sideways, until the woman sidled near and placed a hand on his neck, said words in a strange ancient-sounding language, and he calmed.

The woman dismounted, and Isobell followed suit. "'Twas you guiding us to this place."

"Aye."

"Why?"

"To save you from a fate you dinnae want."

"Being the wife of the MacLachlan?"

"Aye."

What Isobell could only guess was a vision came over her. The green grass on the mound replaced by a cover of the purest white snow. Drops of blood stained the pristine surface. She remembered the bloodstained sheet in the bridal chamber. A trembling took hold of her. She already belonged to Archibald.

"The only way to avert this travesty is to leave this realm for another," the woman said.

"What do you mean?"

"You must leave this place for another. Come with me unto the center of the mound."

If she left she'd never see Archibald again. That thought hurt more than she would have supposed. Isobell closed her eyes, refusing to shed the tears of her heart.

When she felt strong enough to open them again and face the truths of the past night, the vision was gone. She stood with her horse on the mound of green grass. The mysterious woman had vanished.

Isobell stepped back in fear and bumped into Dealanach Dubh. The horse bolted through the curtain of falling snow and into the storm.

She darted after him but the snowdrifts had deepened to her waist. If she continued she'd surely perish. Backtracking, she returned to the grassy knoll, but stayed at its edge, afraid to venture onto the mound itself.

Rumors abounded about places such as this. Stories told by old folk. Stories Isobell had thought were intended to frighten children into behaving.

There were many such tales about the knoll in the Firwood. Legend claimed the place was inhabited by faeries. As a child, she'd marveled over stories of mysterious beams of brightly colored lights hovering over the hill on especially dark, starless nights. A chill skimmed over Isobell's shoulders. They claimed that beneath the hill resided Finvarra, King of the Faeries. She'd heard stories of melodious music coming from below where the king hosted wild gatherings. Some believed he kidnapped beautiful mortal women and forced them below to spend a never ending evening feasting and dancing.

Perhaps there was some truth to the stories. The hill was definitely a place of magic. Wee twinkling stars danced just above the grass and in the single tree at the center of the mound. A tree with an abundance of verdant leaves and fragrant citrus-scented blossoms that shouldn't exist in this place, and certainly not at this time of year.

She cautiously approached, drawn by the twinkling lights glimmering on the unusually green grass. She touched one and it flew away on wings. She took a step back, away from the knoll, turned, and ran into the snow.

An arrow whizzed past her head. Isobell dove back onto the mound. She lingered at its edge for the longest time, chewing on her bottom lip, wondering what to do. How had the other reivers found her during such a dreadful storm? Why hadn't they followed her onto the mound?

Walk to the center of the knoll, Isobell.

More words in that ancient tongue yet this time she understood.

She couldn't help but stroll onto the mound and try to capture one of the wondrous dancing lights. She giggled and forgot to be afraid. She danced in a circle and laughed aloud.

When she reached the center of the mound, she looked at the sky and at the full moon, and her stomach quivered.

Nausea made her sway. She grasped her belly as she fell backward into a dark well, falling as if there was no bottom.

Down, down, down, deeper into the black hole. She screamed but heard no sound.

Her body spun…or was the hole spinning? She couldn't think. Pain exploded behind her eyes. A sharp white beam of light appeared afore her and on instinct, she followed it. What would she find there? Before she could find out, she burst into a cloudy sky and dropped ever so slowly, landing with a soft thud on snow-covered ground.

Isobell clutched the cloth covering her chest. Her heart felt as if it would gallop away.

Where was she? Nothing looked familiar. She reached over her shoulder and squeezed the leather scabbard strapped to her back. Her sword remained in its sheath. She pulled the blade free and pointed it forward, darting a gaze from left to right, searching for a threat.

She must be somewhere beneath the faerie mound. Finvarra's enchanted world?

She stood in a noble winter garden, but none she'd ever visited. Snow still fell, but in the gentlest of ways, dusting the soil and bushes with glistening sparkles.

"What are you doing here, Isobell?"

CHAPTER SEVEN

Archibald held the ruby ring in a clenched fist, the large stone jabbing his palm. "She's gone? What do you mean she's gone?"

"Keep calm, my Chief." Aine was not intimidated by his bluster. "Dinnae fash. 'Twill make you ill."

Munn wrung his big hands, gaze lowered to the stone floor. "She ran away."

"I gathered that. But why?"

"She refused to stay with a man she hates. Who she foolishly believes did harm to her clan. That father of hers filled her head with lies." Hands on hips, Aine glared at the brownie. "Best be tellin' him the all of it."

Munn released a loud sigh. "I put a potion in her wine to make her forget all the bad things her da told her about you. When you drank from the cup you…"

"Go on."

"You passed out. But before you did, you shook Isobell awake and accused her of poisoning you. The forgetting spell had worn off, and she ran away."

"How long has she been gone?"

"Since before midnight," Aine said. "You will bring her back. Aye?"

Archibald scraped a palm over stiff whiskers. "How long have I slept?"

"'Tis' nearly time for the even' meal."

He paced to the window. Heavy snow pummeled the castle, making it difficult to see the bay clearly and naught beyond. Isobell kenned she hadn't tried to poison him. Why would she risk her life, traveling through a raging storm?

"Anything could have happened to her out there alone, lost in the snow."

"You will find her." Aine had more faith in him than he did.

Isobell could be anywhere. They'd never be able to track her in the snow. He paced back to the hearth. "If the potion wore off for her, if it was nae longer potent, why did it make me pass out?"

Munn frowned and scraped a foot over the floor. "My potions dinnae always work as expected."

"Great! And now my lady-wife is lost in a blizzard."

The brownie hung his head.

"You never should have interfered. 'Twas wrong to give Isobell a potion to forget. With time, I would have convinced her that I am not the evil man her father made me out to be."

"She would have run before you had the chance," Munn shot back.

There was some truth in that. Isobell wouldn't have given him the time he needed. She'd planned to bolt from the beginning. Archibald ran both hands through his thick hair, wanting to tear the strands from his head. Had it not been for the potion, she never would have signed the contract and said the vows.

Though she wouldn't have run during a raging storm. She had more sense than that.

No matter what she did in the past, she was legally his wife, and thereby he had every right to find her and bring her back. He had to believe she would survive her folly of running away into the storm and that he would find her and bring her home where she belonged. With him.

56

The lull to which Archibald woke was short lived. By gloaming, the storm intensified with high winds screaming over Loch Fyne and battering the castle walls. Visibility outside became nil, inside the mood of the clan downright gloomy.

The fierce weather lasted two more days and nights. On the third day, dawn greeted the castle with a calm, clear, sunny sky. The air much warmer. Melting snow dripped from roofs and slush made the courtyard and paths slippery. Ropes used to pull boats back and forth over the slushy ice of the bay had been secured prior to the storm, but weren't needed. Archibald and a small contingent of men, including Munn, crossed to the mainland with little difficulty and set out after Isobell on horseback.

With no tracks to follow, Archibald could only guess as to where she would go. If she thought to be accused of poisoning him, she'd need to hide well. If he were on the run, avoiding a probable death sentence, he would head to Glasgow and seek passage to France.

Would she do the same?

The burgh was as good a place as any to start the search. 'Twas also a great place to hide.

Drifts of melting snow and mud on trails made traveling difficult. Scouts trudged ahead, swept the area to the left and right, and returned with naught to report. With each step, Archibald prayed she'd found safe haven from the storm.

"There is a large animal moving yonder." Duncan pointed to a massive thicket.

Archibald signaled two of the lads forward. They disappeared from sight, but shortly one reappeared and whistled for the others to proceed. The second lad led Isobell's black stallion from behind the gnarly clump of bushes and small trees, and Archibald's stomach and hopes plummeted.

"Is there any sign of my lady-wife?"

One lad struggled with the agitated beast. The other shook his head.

The curse came from deep within Archibald's soul—guttural and vile. He stomped away from the lads and cursed some more.

A series of birdcalls signaled the return of a scout. The lad approached, carrying one of Archibald's *plaides*.

Archibald squeezed the wool in a clenched fist and brought it to his nose. The scent of lavender lingered on the cloth. Isobell had certainly crossed this area. She must have taken the *plaide* before leaving their bedchamber. "Where did you find this?"

"On far knoll." The man pointed and frowned. "A hill of greenest grass that looks as if 'twas never touched by the storm."

"The accursed *Sithichean Sluaigh?*" Archibald shot a stern look at Munn. "What do you ken of this?"

He shrugged yet knowledge and guilt shone on his weathered brown face.

Archibald pivoted to face Duncan. "Return with the lads to the castle."

"Aye, I will send them back, but permit me to remain. I am well aware of fae activity in this area."

Archibald's eyes widened. "Are you now?"

Duncan solemnly nodded. "Lady Laurie demanded I escort her to the *Sithichean Sluaigh* when she ran from Patrick's planned marriage for her to another. She claimed from there she could return home. At the time, I thought her a faerie. Now I ken otherwise. Still, there is something magical about that damned knoll. Perhaps Finn MacIntyre's claims are truth."

"That is difficult to believe. The lad lived in a fantasy world of his own making."

"Aye, difficult to be sure. Yet…"

"Send the lads home and we will explore the knoll."

With Munn standing on the back of Archibald's horse, they rode to the *Sithichean Sluaigh*, the infamous faerie hill. They dismounted, and searched the area, avoiding stepping onto the knoll itself, but found naught to prove Isobell had been there.

"Look at this." Duncan squatted and picked up a nicked arrow.

Archibald's throat thickened, making it difficult to swallow. Had the reivers found Isobell and had she ran onto the knoll and... He glowered at Munn. "How does the knoll work?"

"Dinnae ken. Only the fae ken its secrets."

"Yet Lady Laurie believed she could magically travel from this spot?"

"Aye. But not at will."

"And where exactly would a person travel to from here?"

Munn's throat worked. He scanned the hill and the surrounding area as if he thought others might be near. He stepped close to Archibald and whispered, "To other realms, to the past, to the future."

"Ach, I must be as mad as the village idiot to consider this." Archibald handed his reins to Duncan. "If I can make this work, send a messenger to Glasgow requesting Suibhne return home from university at the earliest opportunity. Until he arrives, you are in charge of the castle and clan."

He strode to the center of the knoll, shoulders back, jaw set. Waited. Naught happened. He made fists and waited. Naught. "What am I doing wrong?"

Munn shrugged. "Workings of the faerie hill are a mystery."

"Perhaps 'tis the weapons," Duncan offered. "Mayhap they put off the fae."

"*Grrrr!* I dislike traveling unarmed." Archibald glanced around. "Dinnae see Isobell's sword anywhere."

With a tilt of the head, Duncan held his hands up, palms forward.

Archibald shrugged off the scabbard securing the claymore to his back and handed them to his man. Then he removed the dirk from his waist and the multiple blades hidden upon his person and dropped them at the edge of the knoll. With a brisk pace, he returned to the center. Still naught happened to take him to Isobell. "Now what?"

"'Tis said the fae have a dislike of iron."

"Duncan, you possess an uncanny wealth of faerie-lore."

The man grinned at the sarcasm, which increased Archibald's frustration, but he removed the pouch from his belt anyway, placed the brooch from his shoulder into it, and removed his belt with its heavy iron buckle, handing the lot to Munn.

He stood, legs apart, hands fisted on hips, in the center of the cursed mound wearing *leine* and *trews*, draped in his *plaide*, and counted to one hundred. Still naught of a magical nature occurred.

"Mayhap you cannot take anything from this time." Archibald didn't care for Duncan's suggestion. Not in the least.

"You jest?" Yet he removed the *plaide*, *leine*, and *trews*, leggings and boots then stood in the center of the knoll butt-naked. And naught happened except his feeling an arse. "'Tis not working."

"Perhaps the timing is wrong. Lady Laurie had wanted to arrive at the knoll by nightfall and on a full moon."

Munn's eyes rounded, then he spun and vanished.

Damn *brunaidh!* Archibald cursed something fierce while dressing and rearming.

"Why dinnae you mention this timing theory before? Though it was not visible because of the storm, there was to be a full moon the night of the wedding. I took it as a good omen. I was wrong." He banged a fist on his thigh. "*Grrrr!* Nearly two fortnights must pass before the next moon grows full."

CHAPTER EIGHT

Present day
Anderson Creek, North Carolina

*I*sobell froze at the sound of the familiar, brusque voice. Eyes of the coldest blue bore into her. Eyes she thought to never see again. *Patrick MacLachlan.*

How could *he* be here in this place of magic?

Archibald's twin, the man from many an anxious dream, strode forward, wearing the strangest garments. Blue *trews* of an unusual cloth and a black tunic, stretched tight over a broad chest, leaving thick arms mostly bare, even though it snowed.

How much he looked like Archibald. Isobell took a step back, clutching the sword.

"Easy." He approached, hands and arms hanging loose at his sides. "Put the sword down, lass."

"Patrick, who's there?" Lady Laurie, also wearing unusual garments though with a *plaide* wrapped around her shoulders, brushed past her husband and stopped abruptly. "Isobell?"

"W-why are you in f-faerieland? I thought you lived in France." Isobell's teeth chattered and then she started to shake. The sword dropped from numb fingers and the lady she once despised for stealing her betrothed enveloped her within comforting arms and hugged her close.

"We need to get her out of the cold, Patrick. Take care of that, will you?" Lady Laurie pointed at the sword lying in the snow. "Come, Isobell, you'll be warmer inside."

They entered a small structure with walls made of glass, full of verdant foliage of an unusual nature, and blooms of many colors—white, green, yellowish-green, cream, yellow, brown, pink, and even red—a marvel for the senses filled with enchanting fragrance.

Moist warmth melted the icy cold of her skin. Isobell snapped shut a gaping mouth. "What is this place?"

Patrick joined them, minus the sword. "Before we go into that, perhaps you can tell us how you came to be here."

"'Tis a long story."

"I am sure." Patrick arched a brow.

"Well, I…" Isobell ran a finger over a smooth leaf, wondering where to begin. Unsure of how much to tell. Perhaps she shouldn't tell them anything. "I think *you* should tell me where we are first."

"Wait. Let me call my father." He retrieved a strange device from within a fold in his *trews* and held it to his mouth. "Da, we have a situation here. Isobell just walked through the garden gate."

Isobell grabbed hold of Lady Laurie's arm and whispered, "Is he addled?"

Lady Laurie uttered a very unladylike snort and shook her head.

Patrick glanced at his wife then returned attention to the device he held. "Aye. We are in the orchid house. Aye. Bring Mairi and, ach, well, she should bring one of Elspeth's baskets. She will ken the one." The *thing* he spoke into disappeared to whence it came.

"Now for your tale, Isobell." He hadn't changed much, his tone demanded as it always had, as if he ordered his warriors.

Lady Laurie's arm came around her. "Don't let him intimidate you. Come and sit."

She ushered Isobel into the center of the chamber to four iron chairs with green cushions circling a low iron table with an amazing glass top, and then encouraged her to sit. Patrick sat on the other side of the table, Lady Laurie to her left.

"Well." Patrick leaned forward, hands on knees.

"Stop growling at her. Remember what it felt like when you first came here." His wife squeezed Isobell's hand. "Take your time and tell us what you can."

Maybe she should just tell them and get it over with. "My father betrothed me to Archibald, but I did not want to wed him so I ran away."

"I thought you wanted to be his wife," Patrick snapped.

His wife sent him a glare. "If you can't be pleasant, you should leave."

"I am sorry, Isobell. 'Tis just your presence here has left me unsettled."

She inclined her head, accepting the apology. Patrick had changed much. There was less tension around his eyes. And he apologized. Incredibly unexpected.

"My father had told me of horrible deeds Archibald inflicted on our clan."

"Archie?" Lady Laurie and Patrick asked in unison.

"Aye. Crimes perpetrated against the clan. Raids. Killings. Rapes."

"That does not sound like Archie," Patrick said.

"Do you think perhaps your father lied?" Lady Laurie said, in a gentle, non-accusing tone.

Da would never lie to her. Or would he? Was it possible? Da had been in a rage over Patrick's marriage to Lady Laurie. Could she have been wrong to listen to Da's ranting? He *had* forgiven Archibald rather quickly once he received the signed betrothal contract.

"I was horrified. I ran. Archibald found me, and they tried to force me to the altar, but I refused, and they locked me up."

"You poor thing."

Isobell squirmed. She didn't deserve Lady Laurie's

sympathy. "The MacLachlan clan brownie—"

"*Grrr!*" Patrick glowered. "What did Munn do?"

"Well, he gave me wine to drink that made me forget things. Made me forget I hated Archibald. I signed the contract and said the vows and we consummated the marriage."

The wine made her forget about the numerous raids too. Maybe it would have been better if she hadn't remembered.

"So you are Archibald's wife," Patrick said. "Does he ken how you came to be here?"

"Oh, nae!" She rubbed tired eyes.

"You must be exhausted," Lady Laurie said.

"Aye."

"We should retire to the house."

"Da and Mairi are on the way." Patrick leaned back in the chair, hands clasped behind his head, feet crossed at the ankle.

"There is more. Archibald believes I poisoned him," Isobell blurted. "I did not."

"What? My son poisoned?" The gruff voice made Isobell jump. The scowl on Iain MacLachlan's face made it difficult to swallow.

"You are supposed to be dead." She clasped a hand over her mouth, horrified.

"Hah. Never felt better." He slapped a fist to his chest. "Does my son live?"

"Aye." She nodded, feeling a wee bit dizzy.

"Hello, my dear, 'tis lovely to see you." Lady Mairi bustled into the room with a basket hanging over a wrist and wearing a short, blue gown with a shorter, matching jacket over top. My goodness, more than her ankles showed.

Isobell hopped up then dropped into a curtsy and held. "Thank you, Lady Mairi."

"Get up, lass. And just call me Mairi. We dinnae hold much with formality here."

"In faerieland?"

"This is nae faerieland." Iain scoffed. "What of my son?"

"He snored loud enough to wake the dead last I saw him." Isobell swallowed uneasily. "What do you mean nae faerieland?"

Mairi patted her hand. "Nae worries. We will take care of you."

"If I am not in faerieland, where am I?" Her gaze leapt from one person to another, seeking an answer yet fearing what it might be.

"The future. The twenty-first century," Iain said.

"You will get used to it," Patrick said.

Isobell looked to the right. To the left. Her heart raced. She wanted to run, but to where?

"Leave be. You've got her panicking. Isobell has had a trying experience." Lady Laurie clasped Isobell's hand. "We should let her rest. She can tell us how she came to be here in the morning. And she'll share all the news from Castle Lachlan. Won't you, Isobell?"

She nodded.

"We'll take her to the inn." Mairi smiled sweetly.

"I don't think a ride in a car is a good idea yet. She can have something to eat and stay in our guest room. Will that suit, Isobell?"

"Aye." What other choice did she have?

Lady Mairi held out the basket to Lady Laurie. "One of Elspeth's remedies is in here. Something calming for Isobell to drink."

"Nae. I dinnae want another potion."

"Another? Hmmm." Patrick's forehead furrowed and he rubbed his chin.

"I'm sure she'll be fine without it," Lady Laurie said.

Lady Mairi and… What should she call Iain? Since he is alive, is he the MacLachlan or is Archibald chief? This whole affair was too confusing. The older couple left through one door, and she, Lady Laurie, and Patrick through the door to the garden. They crossed the snow dusted courtyard and entered a much larger structure into a small chamber with coats hanging on hooks and boots on a mat on the floor—

some *bairn*-sized—and into a...kitchen perhaps.

"Lady Laurie? My sword?"

"Please just call me Laurie."

"Put away for safe keeping," Patrick said. "We would not want anyone to get hurt by mistake."

Or on purpose. "I ken how to use it."

"That is of interest. How did you come by such skill, Isobell?"

"Can the two of you call a truce?" Lady Laurie's fists were on her hips and she glowered at her husband. "Let's leave what's in the past in the past."

Patrick responded with an abrupt nod and refrained from further comment.

Isobell was more than thankful she wasn't wed to Patrick.

What of the man to whom she was wed? Had he survived the suspected poison? One moment he was fine. More than fine. Heat stole up her chest as she thought of what they'd done in the marriage bed. The next, he accused her of poisoning him.

If she hadn't been the one, then who?

"I need to go back and find out if Archie is all right and learn who gave him the poison. Tell me how to return home."

"Whoa. Slow down, Isobell," Patrick said. "If he truly snored when you left him, I doubt he was poisoned."

"You do care for him." Lady Laurie grinned.

"If he wasn't poisoned, why would he accuse me of such?"

"He must have believed it at the time. Laurie is right. We all need sleep. Tomorrow, you will tell us the entire tale and we will figure out how best to deal with whatever has happened." Patrick folded his arms over his chest. The chief had spoken. Or whatever he was now.

"Ignore him." Laurie opened a door on the front of a very large, shiny, silver box. "You will find this time has wonderful conveniences. This is the refrigerator; it's a cold box, where we keep perishable foods. If you feel hungry during the night, feel free to help yourself to whatever you find."

"Thank you." Wondrous indeed.

Laurie placed a hunk of cheese and an apple on a small plate and handed it to Isobell. Then she poured something from an odd-shaped pitcher into a mug. Isobell sniffed the drink. It smelled like the spiced cider she was used to at home.

There were other unusual furnishings in the chamber, but she could learn more about them at another time. She did need to sleep to get her strength back.

They climbed wide, straight steps to a second floor. 'Twas incomprehensible that Patrick would live in such an indefensible home.

Laurie stopped in front of a doorway and faced Isobell with a smile. "We light our chambers with…special lamps. Switches just inside turn them on and off." She reached inside and pushed a wee knob up. Light drenched the chamber afore them.

Isobell jumped back. Then she stepped forward, reached inside the door, and pushed the knob down. The chamber went dark. She flicked it up—light. She felt her grin all the way to her toes. What a marvelous place—faerieland.

"'Tis a lovely chamber." Like naught she'd ever seen. The walls were pale yellow with curtains that had flowers on them. A rug of blue and gold wool graced the polished wood floor. Such a luxury to have wood floors instead of cold stone. The large bed took up most of the room and had many plump pillows, and puffy linens that matched the curtains.

There was no fireplace yet the chamber was warm. How could that be?

"There is a bathroom—a bathing chamber through the other door. Come I'll show you how it works."

Laurie placed the tray on a table next to the bed and led the way into the bathing chamber. Isobell trailed fingers over the bedding in passing, looking forward to sleeping in the big bed. In the bathing chamber, she had to cover her mouth with a hand to muffle a gasp. Everything was white, except for fluffy yellow and blue drying cloths. And shiny silver spigots.

"You'll get used to it." Laurie chuckled. "The knobs on the right are for cold water, left for hot."

Isobell watched the demonstration in awe. She doubted she'd ever get used to such wonders. Such luxury.

Laurie reached an arm behind a glass wall. "The shower works with a twist of this knob. Part way is cold. All the way is hot. I usually prefer it in the middle like this."

Water rained from a large square spigot just above head level. Wondrous indeed.

"This is the toilet, like in the garderobe at Castle Lachlan, but better. After you, you know, press this knob and, you know, everything flushes away." Laurie demonstrated.

Isobell giggled. "May I use it now?"

"Of course. I'll wait out there until you're done."

When Isobell returned to the bedchamber, Laurie looked up from her perch on the bed. "I hope you'll let me be your friend. I understand that the MacLachlan men can try your patience on occasion. I don't believe Archie is the monster your father made him out to be. From my experience, he is a good man."

Isobell nodded, but could she trust the woman?

"I'll leave so you can eat." Laurie rose and walked to the door then looked back. "I'll bring you a clean nightgown."

Isobell plopped onto the bed and devoured the fruit and cheese. Before she finished the cider, Laurie returned.

"Here. It's hardly been worn." The woman blushed.

Heat scorched Isobell's cheeks too. "Thank you. I appreciate your kindness."

"I know what it's like to find yourself in a time not your own."

"But faerieland…"

"Iain told the truth. This is not faerieland. It's the future where I came from before I landed in your time and met Patrick."

"Oh."

"Sleep well." Laurie left her alone.

Isobell doubted she'd be able to sleep. The future... Was it possible?

Using the shower in the bathing chamber was a delight. She donned the borrowed nightgown and slid between crisp sheets. Patrick must be very wealthy in this time to afford such luxury.

The thought of Patrick brought thoughts of Archibald. Had she been wrong to believe Da? Would Archie forgive her if she returned to him? If she could return to him?

Did she want to return to him?

CHAPTER NINE

*I*sobell woke slowly, rays of sunlight warming her face. Then she startled. She was in a strange bed. In a strange chamber. In a strange house. She trembled with a flash of memory—faerieland. Or was it the future?

A gown of sorts draped a wooden chair in the corner. Isobell padded to the chair barefooted, surprised to find the floor warm to the touch. Standing in front of an incredibly clear looking-glass, she donned the drab gray dress—not to her taste—and slipped into the leather shoes tucked beneath the chair.

Inhaling a deep, calming breath, she descended the stairs. After crossing through several amazing chambers, with wonders beyond her ken, she found the kitchen. Laurie sat at a table speaking with a redheaded woman whose back was to Isobell. She halted, hesitant to interrupt.

"Why should the Chief of Clan MacLachlan's happiness matter to me? My only concern is the queen's challenge," the woman said.

"What ken you of Archibald?" Isobell marched into the kitchen.

The woman spun around, green eyes narrowed.

"You!" Isobell blurted, startled to recognize the woman.

A furrow crossed Laurie's brow. "You've met Caitrina?"

"Oh, aye." Isobell fisted hands on hips. "She came to my...cottage. Claimed to ken my destiny."

Caitrina frowned. "Just how exactly did you come to be here?"

"Isobell, please sit. Perhaps you can tell us the whole tale now, while the men are out of the way, practicing swordplay."

When Isobell finished with the telling, Caitrina's neck and face flushed red.

"I can hardly believe Munn told the truth. Oonagh has interfered. She led Isobell to the faerie hill and brought her forward through the gate. Why?"

"Who is Oonagh?" Isobell asked.

"The Queen of the Fae."

"Why would she interfere with Isobell and Archie?" Laurie asked.

"I dinnae ken. But she has." Caitrina pursed her lips. "I need to leave."

The woman stood and left through the door to the garden. Isobell followed and peered out the window. Then clutched her chest.

"Oh my!" The woman walked just beyond the garden gate and vanished into the mist. Isobell dropped onto a chair. "She is a faerie?"

"She is, but this isn't faerieland."

"Then why are there faeries here?"

"Because they are everywhere." Laurie sighed. "Let's forget the faeries for a moment. We should talk about you and Archie. You're wed. You need to work out your differences. We'll find a way to send you back."

"What if I dinnae want to go?"

"You care for Archie. Don't you owe it to him and to yourself to learn the truth?"

She wanted to, but even if her father had lied, there was no future for her and Archibald. He'd never forgive her for the year she'd spent raiding, seeking revenge against him and his clan.

When he learned the extent of her betrayal, he'd seek justice for his clan. She swallowed uneasily. He had every right to condemn her to death by hanging.

❀ ❀ ❀

Castle Lachlan, 1512

Munn felt the pull of Caitrina's summons. The darn faerie had a lot of nerve bothering him while he attended his chief. Choosing to ignore the compulsion, he planted his feet firmly on the straw-covered floor. The itchy rash started on his chest then spread. He kenned better than to scratch. It would just make the eruption worse. He squirmed, wiggled, did a shimmy.

"What is the matter with you?" Archibald frowned.

Too uncomfortable to answer, Munn gritted his teeth. Sweat prickled the folds in his forehead. Archibald, and the two lads assisting him, took several steps back as if Munn had gone raving mad. He couldn't hold out much longer. The annoying faerie's call too strong.

Without conscious thought, he spun and disappeared from the stable, traveling sideways through the ether. Nausea clenched his stomach muscles. Inhaling sharply, he curled into a ball, landing as such, and rolled across the green grass, stopping at Caitrina's dainty feet.

"You foolish, wee man. You thought to ignore me?"

How dare she? Munn hissed, ready to curse her from here to there.

"Whist! There is nae time for theatrics." Caitrina's shoulders slumped. "As much as I hate to admit it, you were right. The queen has taken interest in Archibald and Isobell."

"Why?"

"Probably naught but a whim." The faerie's pointed ears twitched and her eyes flared as if listening to something only she could hear. She frowned, cursed, and then returned attention to Munn. "Seems Fate suggests a Christmas Eve conceiving."

"Oonagh and Fate dinnae get along."

"Nae, they do not. Oonagh believes she has placed Isobell out of the MacLachlan's reach and has demanded we accept a side challenge."

"We? Nae we."

"You will help. If we win this challenge, the queen promises not to interfere in the third match of the original challenge. You want Archibald and Isobell to be happy. Aye?"

Munn nodded. He did want the chief to be happy, but the chief was still mad about the enchanted wine.

"Then see to it Archibald is on the faerie hill this night."

Munn glanced at the cloud filled sky. "There is not to be a full moon this night."

"I ken. I will guide him through the gate."

"The queen will place obstacles in the way."

"Aye. She will."

Munn shuddered. He didn't wish to feel the queen's wrath again.

"'Tis up to you to ensure the MacLachlan line lives beyond Archibald." Caitrina pinned him with a green stare.

"But..."

"Remember your duty is to the MacLachlan clan." She vanished.

Present day
Anderson Creek, North Carolina

"How can I ever learn if my da spoke the truth when he condemned Archie, or if he spoke falsely?" Isobell plopped onto the sofa next to Laurie and her *bairn*. "If I ask him, he'll claim he never said those things. Since I am now married to Archie, Da wants me to submit and have children that will be born of the blood of both clans. Those who corroborated his previous tales will back his new position."

"There is a way." Iain stood in the doorway, wee lads in tow, wooden swords held in pudgy fists.

The lads had angelic faces, eyes wide with curiosity, but they were more than likely mischievous devils. Isobell rubbed her chest near her heart. She'd always wanted to have children. She'd lied to Archie about making sure he'd have no heir.

Isobell jerked her attention back to Iain. "How can I learn the truth?"

"A trip to the library in Asheville. The library has a written history of the MacLachlan clan. It details the progression of the feud."

"And there are online sources that would detail the Lamont side of the story," Laurie patted Isobell's hand. "You're going to get your first ride in a car."

"I want to go too," Young Iain declared.

"Me too!" Scott, said with a jounce.

Iain scrunched down to the level of the twins. "You dinnae like the library because it requires quiet, but if your ma agrees, we will bring you something back from the candy store. Besides, Nana plans to put out more Christmas decorations. I am sure she will let you help."

The lads turned puppy dog eyes on their mother. Laurie nodded, and the children twirled together in a merry dance then scooted from the chamber shouting war cries. The wee lass in Laurie's arms fussed, wanting to chase after her brothers.

"I'm not sure Mairi will appreciate the boys' interference."

Iain chuckled. "She adores the lads and will be happy to have their assistance."

Laurie rolled her eyes. "Let me put the little lady down for a nap and call a babysitter. Then we'll take a scenic drive along the Blue Ridge Parkway to Asheville. The views will remind you of home."

Isobell donned the embellished skinny jeans and red cashmere sweater Laurie purchased for her and tugged on soft napped ankle boots. With a toss of her hair over a shoulder and a glance in the looking-glass, she smiled. The garments felt strange, tighter than what she was used to, but she liked the way she looked. *Almost like a local.*

The snow on her arrival had been short-lived. The air now warm. Laurie called it a late Indian summer. 'Twas pleasant. Isobell strolled through the garden, waiting to take her first journey in this very strange future.

Iain returned after what felt like forever with a large, shiny-black, covered cart. No horse required to pull it. Amazing indeed. Isobell sat on the back bench with Laurie, and Patrick in the front with his da.

The drive was uneventful. Who kenned why the others thought she'd be unnerved? The vehicle progressed along a black, hard-packed trail in silence. Spectacular views from the windows left her awed. The land was much like Scotland with its mountains and heavy mists, but with so many more trees, bare now of leaves.

She hesitated before entering the building in the bustling town of Asheville, her stomach doing a little flip. The others regarded her with solemn eyes.

"I dinnae want to learn anything beyond what happened the day I left. I would rather not ken Archibald's future." *Or mine.*

"We understand. That is wise." Iain took hold of her elbow and escorted her into the library. A marvel, full of more books than she thought existed. He'd reserved a private gathering chamber where they sat at a square wooden table with four wooden chairs. Laurie fetched the books in question and read from the text since Isobell was unable to read the writing of their time. 'Twas true. From the book's account, Da had lied.

Then Laurie read from a marvelous thing displaying all sorts of images. They called it a computer. The Lamont account of the feud was somewhat different than that of the MacLachlans, but still held Archie innocent.

Isobell didn't ken whether to be happy or sad to have

been so misled. And by Da. He had been very good to her as a child. Providing for her every desire. But when she refused to wed those chosen for her, he became a stubborn goat.

"Well, daughter. What do you plan to do now?" Iain—her father-in-law—asked.

Her eyes misted. She didn't deserve his affection.

Would he and the rest of the family shun her when they learned of her participation in the wrongful raids against their clan in the past?

CHAPTER TEN

Fir-wood, 1512

An arrow whizzed past Archibald's head. "The Lamont renegades are not that good of marksmen. Why all of a sudden are their shots coming close to the mark?"

"The faerie queen. She interferes," Munn shouted over the thunder of pounding hoofs.

Fae intervention? Archibald didn't care for the implication, but perhaps he was becoming a believer.

And just where the hell had Maclay come from? The man was supposed to be dead.

Archibald urged his horse to greater speed. The brownie cursed, but remained standing at his back. Archibald planned to brave the knoll this night. He wouldn't allow flying arrows or the living-dead to stop him from traveling to Isobell.

"Make a run for it," Duncan, riding beside him, yelled. "Me and the lads will waylay the damn reivers and that bastard Maclay."

The men pulled back, and Archibald continued the furious race for the mound. The steed balked at the edge of the knoll, and he dropped to the ground. Munn jumped to his side.

"Dash home, lad." He slapped the horse's rump and the

beast bolted back the way they'd come. He hoped the horse made it past the reivers and to its stall in the stable before another bout of bad weather set in. Though he couldn't worry about that now. He'd more important travel on his mind.

The knoll was much the same as on their last visit except for the suspect sparkling lights hovering over the grass and in the branches of the one tree at its center. A tree that wasn't there the other day. And shouldn't display leaves at this time of year. He shivered. Unnerved by the knoll's unpredictable behavior. "Now what?"

Munn muttered something that sounded like, *"Where is the darn faerie?"* then marched to the center of the mound. "Stand here."

With each step, Archibald felt an unusual pull. A humming in his head. Mist wrapped around his legs, slithering and swirling. When nausea hit, he grabbed Munn's arm, and they both fell backward, dropping into a black pit. Down, down, down. Faster and faster.

"What in the—" The words were lost amidst the sound of a howling wind. Please, not the cry of *banshees.* Harbingers of death.

They plunged for what seemed like forever. *Where would this mad journey end?*

Archibald lost grasp of Munn as they spun, or mayhap the pit was spinning. He didn't ken which. Colors flashed fitfully. So dizzy he wanted to vomit, he grabbed hold of a beckoning white light and followed it through the mayhem of his mind. *Take me to Isobell.*

He shot into a star-filled night sky and tumbled head over heels several times until he hit a barrier that felt like a huge spider web. Stuck like a fly. His skin crawled, panic setting in, but then the thing released him and he drifted to the ground, landing on all fours. *Grumpf!* Munn landed beside him on his arse with a loud grunt.

"Did we make it?" Archibald demanded.

"Nice position, brother mine."

Archibald leapt to his feet, fists ready for defense. No risk of attack. His twin stood afore him with a wide grin as if the misery he felt a fine joke. Patrick presented a hand. They grasped forearms as warriors then embraced as brothers of the womb.

"I was not supposed to travel too," Munn grumbled. "Caitrina will rage at me."

Archibald chuckled along with his brother. Relief made him almost giddy. The *Sithichean Sluaigh* hadn't sent him into the fires of hell or some equally horrific place.

"You can handle her, imp," Patrick said, distracting Archibald from the uncomfortable thoughts of what could have happened.

"As glad as I am to see you, I came to find Isobell," he said.

"She is here. Safe in the house with Laurie."

"Thank the good Lord. Take me to her."

"Not yet. We need to talk first. We can go to my study." Patrick glanced in Munn's direction. "Come along, wee man."

Archibald followed his twin through a gate into a well-tended winter garden and into a massive wooden structure.

"Welcome to the home I built." Patrick's face lit with pride.

Archibald understood his brother taking pleasure in the dwelling. As they proceeded through several different chambers, he hid an acute curiosity, a desire to learn how things worked, keeping in mind the reason for being here—though he wasn't sure where here was—to fetch Isobell and return home. Munn had no such compunction, he touched everything in passing until Patrick slapped his fingers and bade him stop.

They retired to the well-appointed study. Archibald smiled. Patrick had reproduced the study at Castle Lachlan though this chamber displayed even more wealth.

Patrick stepped to the hearth and withdrew a multifaceted glass flagon, pouring the amber liquid into two matching glasses. "I imagine you could use a whisky. I certainly want one."

Archibald collapsed into a chair afore the hearth where a small fire crackled. He took a sip of the offered drink and relished the slow burn in his gut.

"Just where is here?" he asked.

"The future."

"Ah! Da and Mairi?"

"Live nearby."

"So, Finn told the truth."

"Aye." Patrick nodded, eyes creasing with restrained mirth.

"Where is the reprobate?"

His twin laughed. "He and Elspeth are in a foreign place—Africa—visiting with his father, a man who digs in the dirt, searching for ancient relics."

"Truly?"

"Aye," Patrick said. "Old things hold much value in this time. He would enjoy exploring the storage cells at Castle Lachlan."

"I had to lock Isobell in one."

"I am sure 'twas for her own good."

"'Twas." Still, Archibald felt bad for having imprisoned her, even if it was only for a short time. "I will miss seeing Elspeth and Finn."

"They promised to be home by Christmas Eve. Two days from now. The family will want you and Isobell to stay for the festivities, but the gate is fickle, and you must return to your time when you can."

Archibald frowned. "Christmas is weeks away yet."

"Time sometimes warps when you travel through the gate."

"Oh, I see." He sighed and brushed nervous fingers over the fine wood grain of the chair's arm. "You told a falsehood when you claimed to be going to France to live. I kept expecting a missive. Then gave up. It hurt to never hear from you."

"For that, I am sorry. But you must understand now, my

need for secrecy."

"I would not have believed you if you had told me the truth." Archibald leaned forward, hands on knees, and hung his head. He and Isobell didn't belong in this time and place. They needed to go home where things made sense. He raised his gaze to his brother. "Do you think we will be able to return to our time?"

"We really dinnae ken the workings of the gate. The fae have some control over it, aye, but destiny seems to be a strong pull too. Da believes if a soul comes here then returns to the past, then they cannot come here again. But I doubt that is an issue for you."

"Nae. It is not. I want to take Isobell home where we belong and stay there."

Isobell strolled down the hall, headed for Patrick's study. She wanted him to order a few more things from online. She glanced down at her feet and chuckled, loving the furry, leopard print slippers, the black, silky jammie bottoms, and the warm, hot pink hoodie Laurie had procured for her. The door was open so she entered without knocking and stopped dead.

Archie sat in the chair across from Patrick at the desk.

How? She wanted to back up, pretend she never entered. Find a hole to hide in. Disappear into mist like Caitrina. Run. Instead she closed a gaping mouth and sat in the empty chair next to her husband.

He looked good. Handsome. She wanted to reach out and touch his dear face. Oh, good Lord, what should she say?

Archie stared at her, seemingly also at a loss for words.

She stole a glance at Patrick. His lips quivered. Damn the man.

"I shall leave the two of you alone to—" He chuckled, hurried out of the chamber, and closed the door.

Great. Now what?

They both started to speak at the same time.

"Sorry." She cleared her throat. "You were about to say?"

"You first."

"I would rather you speak first."

He nodded gravely. "None of what your father told you about me was true."

Was she ready to disclose she kenned the truth? "I may have been hasty to believe him, but the tales were terribly gruesome and his lads corroborated the stories."

"Of course they did." Archibald tilted his head to the side, frowned, and raised his gaze heavenward. "They are your father's lads. Can you try to trust me? Give me a chance?"

"Perhaps. I have a confession to make." Not the one she should make, but if they stayed here, he never needed to ken the full truth of her betrayal. "Your da took me to a place of vast knowledge, a library full of books and other wonders. We read about the progression of the feud through the day I left Scotland. My da lied. I ken the truth."

Archie's relief was tangible. She wanted to hug him, but wasn't sure if he'd welcome her forwardness. She moistened dry lips "Do you ken what happened to Dealanach Dubh?"

He cleared his throat with an awkward grind. "Nae worries, sweetling, your fine steed is probably munching hay in his stall in our stables at this verra moment."

Overjoyed, she forgot her insecurity and leapt onto his lap. The chair groaned. She didn't care if they broke it. Isobell threw her arms around Archie's neck and kissed him hard on the mouth.

"Ach, lass, now that is what I call a proper greeting from one's lady-wife."

She had to agree. He felt good. Virile. He smelled good. Fir and fresh air. He wore a clean *leine* and *plaide* with nothing else. A thrill ran through her. Patrick looked handsome in his future garments, but Archie was magnificent in traditional Highland garb.

Isobell wiggled her bum, feeling his desire in all its glory.

He stood her up abruptly, rose from the chair, and grasped both of her hands, holding them out to the side.

With his forehead pressed against hers, he inhaled several quick breaths. Then he leaned back and stared at her.

She could easily get lost in the depths of his molten, silver eyes.

"You are much different in these strange garments." His admiring gaze stroked up and down. "Go and change into proper attire so we can return home."

What? "I dinnae want to return to the past. I want to stay here."

"Nae!" He growled.

She pulled away from him. Fisted her hands. "Aye."

CHAPTER ELEVEN

Archibald paced the confines of Da's study. Aye, he was overjoyed to see Da and Mairi, and ken they were safe, but he had what amounted to an insurmountable problem. Isobell didn't want to return home. She wanted him to stay here in the future.

Impossible. She was daft. This was no place for them. Their lives were in the past.

Da sat behind his desk, hands steepled on the polished surface, ever patient. "Have you considered staying?"

He stopped pacing. "My first duty is to the clan. They need me, especially with Maclay and the renegade Lamont reivers still on the loose."

"You make me proud, son."

His chest expanded. "Thank you. I am glad you approve."

"'Tis a shame, we thought Finn killed Maclay."

"Aye. The devil must have only been injured from the fight and from the fall off the cliff. When our lads checked from above, he appeared dead. I am guessing his renegade followers found him and someone nursed him back to health."

"You need to woo her."

"Who? Isobell? We dinnae have time for such frivolity.

You are as daft as she."

"Nae. Your courtship was fraught with unpleasantries, dealing with the Lamont and misunderstandings between you and Isobell. You ken a woman wants romance."

Archibald ran a hand through his hair. "We dinnae have time for wooing."

"If the gate plans to allow you to return, a couple of days will not matter. You cannot force Isobell to go. She must want to join you. Take time to woo her. Convince her to leave with you after Christmas Eve midnight services."

"Is this a ploy to get us to stay for the family gathering?"

Da's lips quirked. "Of course, we would love to have you both share the holiday meal and festivities with us, but nae, I would not risk the wrath of the faeries or the gate. I firmly believe you need be in accord with your wife or the gate will not work for you. And you will both remain here."

Archibald cursed under his breath. He and Isobell were at an impasse. She wanted to stay. He wanted to return home. Perhaps Da was right—

"Do you ken why she wants to stay?" Da's question broke into his thoughts.

"What does it matter? She is my lady-wife. She belongs with me."

"I am sure the reason means a great deal to Isobell."

Archibald scratched his chin. It probably did. "Ach, well, look at this place. The luxury. I cannot offer such in our time."

"I dinnae think it's about nice things. Have you thought that perhaps she is afraid to go back?"

"Why would she be afraid?"

"How much do you ken about her participation in the raids?"

"She was seen at the scene of the last raid." He pinned Da with a questioning look. "Raids? You think she has been involved in more than one?"

He shrugged. "How would you feel to learn she was verra involved?"

"Do you ken something I dinnae?"

"I am only suggesting you consider the possibility that she was more involved than you ken and fears your reaction."

Archibald dropped into a chair. Why hadn't he thought of that? If they couldn't keep her involvement a secret, he might be forced to bring judgment against her, the penalty could be death by hanging. A flogging and a life of laborious servitude at the least.

The image of Isobell tied to a post, stripped to the waist. Ivory skin exposed to all. Her beautiful hair sheared. A pained flinch and cry when the whip struck. He gripped the armrests of the chair. He couldn't bear it.

If that was to be their destiny, they would both be better off if she remained with his family in this future place. "Da, what do you ken? Please tell me."

"I have read all the accounts available of reiver activity in the area. I believe Maclay and the Lamont renegades were responsible for the raids against both clans, us and the Lamonts. There is a tale about an unnamed lass who led them. A legend of sorts. Historians question its validity. My guess is that Isobell is the unnamed lass."

"She would have never thieved from Lamonts."

Da held up a hand. "Agreed. She may have only kenned about and participated in the raids against you and our clan."

Archibald shook his head. Could Isobell have hated him so much? *Aye.* "Isobell was given to believe I led the raids against the Lamonts."

"Guessed as much." Da's expression turned grim. "What will you do?"

"Dinnae ken." Archibald slapped a palm against his thigh.

"Isobell's name is not mentioned anywhere connected to the raids in the accounts. Either you struck it from the record or no one ever learned of her involvement."

Thank the good Lord. "If what you say is true, if she led the raids, she should be punished. What should I do?"

"Forgive her."

He nodded. Though he wasn't in full agreement. Her

allegiance with her clan was appropriate and she'd believed her actions righteous. Still...

"Revenge for the sake of revenge is wrong," he thought aloud.

"Perhaps you can find a way for her to make amends."

Archibald pursed his lips and considered many options and came up with naught.

"Go and find your wife. Convince her, gently, with tenderness, that she belongs with you in the past."

He wasn't feeling particularly gentle and certainly not tender. Archibald stalked through the back garden, through the woods, and across the meadow to Patrick's house. Isobell wasn't in any of the main floor chambers. In frustration, he searched the garden then found her in the glass house working with Laurie, potting plants.

The glass house was an amazing place. Moist heat kept the plants thriving though the weather outside had turned cold. He wished he could build such a structure at Castle Lachlan. Perhaps his progeny would someday.

If he left Isobell behind, he wouldn't have any progeny. No one else could take her place in his heart. Her essence burned in his soul. He needed to learn the truth. "Isobell, may I have a word with you in private?"

She smiled, put on a jacket, and followed him into the garden.

"Tell me everything that happened the year you were missing."

Her lips curved down. "Can we just forget that time?"

"Nae. There is much I need to understand."

"It doesn't matter what I have done. You will never forgive me for my betrayal against you. Will you?"

"I dinnae ken." He shook his head. "I just dinnae ken." He pivoted and left her standing in the gray garden, looking forlorn. Perhaps she was right. Perhaps he couldn't forgive her.

He brooded over the circumstances of his life for the remainder of the day and evening, and when he came to a decision, he went in search of Munn. He found the imp in Patrick's house sitting on the floor playing with the children. His wee niece stood, wobbled, and threw her arms about Archibald's legs. "Daddy."

The one word was like a dagger to the heart. He wanted to be a da. If he left without Isobell that would never be. His younger brother Suibhne would be his heir.

Fine. He would harden said heart. "Come, Munn. 'Tis time to return to our time."

He wouldn't tell the family he was leaving. They would attempt to stop him. He hoped they'd understand in time. He strode from the house through the courtyard to the back and just beyond the garden gate.

There was no mist this night. A half-moon shone brightly from a clear night sky. Archibald felt naught unusual as he stepped onto the mound. No fae-like pull of any kind. He glared at Munn, who had followed at his heel. "Make it work."

"Cannot."

"Why not?" he managed to get the question out through gritted teeth.

"Will only work when you are ready."

"I am ready now." Though that wasn't true. All he could think about was Patrick's daughter hugging his leg and gazing at him through Isobell's violet eyes. It wasn't his twin's daughter he imagined. 'Twas his.

He couldn't leave Isobell behind. He must convince her to come home with him.

Archibald woke the next morning in the chamber assigned to him, after a fitful night, more confused than ever. He had a lady-wife he loved with all his heart no matter the crime she committed against him, which he could easily forgive, and against his clan, which was not so easily forgiven.

What should he do? He had this one day to find an answer to the dilemma.

CHAPTER TWELVE

*I*sobell tiptoed to the window. Snow dusted the garden and continued to fall in soft, fluffy flakes. Even being lost in the blizzard hadn't destroyed her ability to appreciate the beauty. Fresh snow for Christmas Eve morning. A new beginning for Isobell.

Was it to be here in the future alone or dare she hope Archie would agree to stay?

He'd been especially attentive when he first arrived. Each time their gazes met, he gave her a secret smile that made her heart beat faster. Then yesterday, he questioned her about the past year. His frustration was understandable. He deserved a truthful answer.

Today would be the day of reckoning.

She kept busy during the morning at the inn, helping the women prepare for the feast and decorating a large fir tree with the children. A lovely tradition.

Archie always seemed to be nearby, and she stole covert glances. If he couldn't forgive her, she would probably never see him again after tonight. Her heart ached with the desolate thought.

Loud voices outside the front door brought everyone to a halt. The door swung open and Archie's sister Elspeth stepped in carrying a wee *bairn*. Mairi screeched and ran forward, enveloping the pair in a hug.

A handsome, sandy-haired man crossed the threshold, carrying brightly colored wrapped packages. Must be her husband Finn. The other men approached him, one by one, grasping forearms in a warrior greeting. Finn's eyes flared when Archie presented his arm. Finn pulled him into a manly embrace with much backslapping. "It's good to see you."

"And I, you." Archibald turned to Isobell, grasped her arm and tugged her forward. "Let me present my lady-wife, Lady Isobell."

Flustered, Isobell dropped into an awkward curtsy because of the jeans she was wearing. Finn bowed in a courtly fashion and brought her fingers to his lips.

"We will have none of that, you scoundrel." Archie grabbed her hand away before the kiss. Everyone laughed good-naturedly.

He was jealous. Good. *He should stay with me in the future.* Then she would never need to tell him about her furtive activities of revenge.

Mairi clapped. "Come. Come. Come into the other room."

They headed for the chamber Mairi called the *parlor* where wee lights on the decorated tree sparkled. Gifts were given round. Laurie placed a large box on Isobell's lap.

"What is this?" she asked.

"A Christmas present from me and Patrick. Everyone, including the children, will change into traditional Scottish clothing for midnight service. This is something for you to wear."

"I am touched." Inside the box, Isobell found a woman's linen *leine*, an overdress, and a white-striped wool *arisaid*. She wiped a tear from the side of an eye. "Thank you."

Mugs of warm spiced wine were passed around and the adults enjoyed playing games with the children. Just before dinnertime, the front bell rang and Caitrina entered the inn, brushing snow from her shoulders. A large man with long black hair joined her, carrying more gifts. He towered over

Patrick and Finn who hurried to greet him.

"Douglas, come and meet my son from Scotland, Chief of Clan MacLachlan, and his new wife." Iain signaled him into the parlor where they were introduced.

Isobell shivered. The man's direct gaze seemed to peer inside her. As if he kenned hidden secrets. And she had an awful one she didn't want anyone here to ken. Especially Archie.

Silly. How could Caitrina's friend possibly ken what she'd done? She shook off the odd feeling.

She pressed her lips together. Archie should be told the truth. She hated the way the secret was eating at her insides. Maybe he would forgive her, and they could go home together. Isobell sighed. *Unlikely.*

Caitrina glared at Munn who was playing with the children on the floor. "Who brought the wee brownie?"

"I am afraid it is my fault. I dragged him along with me." Archibald laughed, something Isobell hadn't heard since he became chief. He almost sounded happy.

Caitrina's face reddened, but a whisper from Douglas seemed to calm her.

Isobell watched Archie interact with the others. The men were all powerful in their own right, though Archie was the one that made her heart flutter. She was almost disappointed when Mairi called them to dinner and they were seated in the eating chamber. Unlike the arrangements in the great hall at Castle Lachlan, where the family sat in a line along one side of the head table on the dais, looking out at those seated at the lower tables, everyone here sat around a large table, facing each other. Archie sat in the chair next to her. She looked away. Anywhere so as not to look at him with longing.

Iain stood and held up a glass of wine. "Thank you to our family and friends for being here just in time for a Highland Christmas. Congratulations to Archibald and Isobell on your nuptials. May you have many years of bliss as have Mairi and I."

"Here, here," sounded round the table with a clinking of

glasses.

Isobell shifted uncomfortably, but smiled and nodded at the well-wishers, as did Archie.

Iain sat and glanced at her in challenge. She lowered her gaze not sure what to think.

During dinner Archie's thigh kept brushing hers, and she bit the inside of her lip to avoid reaching over and touching him. Otherwise, dinner became a jovial affair of great food and good conversation, ending with pastry and a hot drink called coffee.

Delectable food and drink—more reasons to remain in this time. If only she could convince Archie to stay too. She rubbed moist palms on her jeans. He would never forgive her. And he wasn't staying.

"Can we make snow angels?" Scott hollered over bantering voices.

"Yes, please," Young Iain begged too.

Laurie urged the lads into jackets and the entire family trudged out into the snowy garden. Patrick flicked a switch. Light illuminated the area, making the snow sparkle. The lads fell onto their backs in the snow, waving their arms and legs. The imprints left behind were the images of angels. Laurie made a large one. Patrick's even larger.

If a once powerful warrior could display a playful side so could she. Isobell dropped onto her back to make an angel of her own. To her utter surprise, Archie threw off his *plaide* and plopped beside her in naught but his *trews* and *leine*. As they spread their arms to make angel wings their fingers touched. Their gazes met. A thrill shot through her.

Archie's eyes flared. He must have felt it too.

She couldn't let the moment pass without making one last memory with him. Isobell squeezed his fingers. "Come with me. I ken a special place."

Archie grabbed his *plaide* and they slipped away from the others frolicking in the snow. She guided him through the inn's garden, along the well-trodden woodland trail, through the meadow and into Laurie's garden and the privacy of the orchid room. Was doubtful the family or guests would visit on this most special of nights—Christmas Eve.

"Why have you brought me here?" he asked.

"Why do you think?" She hoped her smile appeared sensual.

He raised a brow. She pressed against him, grasped his hands and pulled his arms around her, placing them on her bum. His response, a firm squeeze, urged her on. Stretching up onto the balls of her feet, she leaned in and kissed him as sweetly, as passionately, as her heart demanded.

A rough sound erupted from deep within his throat, a growl, a demand, and the kiss intensified into a meeting of mouths and tongues, wet and wild. Isobell's breath came from Archie and his from her. When the fever calmed, forehead resting against forehead, they gasped for air.

"So, that is your answer, lass?"

"Oh, aye!" She melted against him.

He glanced around the small glass chamber then stepped away. He grabbed a cushion from one of the chairs and tossed it on the floor. Then another and another. Using all the cushions, he made a fine bed.

Archie dropped onto the cushions, tested their comfort then offered an inviting hand. "Join me."

She fell on knees on the cushions beside him. Suddenly feeling shy, she tentatively touched his smooth cheek. She had no experience seducing a man.

Archibald wrinkled his nose in the sweetest way. "What?"

"You have been with so many other women. I dinnae ken…"

"Nae so many."

"But Da said—"

"He said a lot of things that were not true. Aye?"

"Aye." She lowered her gaze embarrassed for having believed all the lies.

Archie slid a palm over her hair and down an arm. "I will be gentle."

She didn't want a sedate mating. She wanted it wild like

the serving wenches at Da's keep described. She grasped the bottom edge of Archie's *leine* and ripped it over his head.

His gusty inhale made her laugh. His intense gaze burned. She splayed fingers over his hard chest and licked her dry lips.

The throaty groan that rumbled as he flipped her onto her back made her insides pulse. Before she had another thought, her sweater was tossed onto a chair and Archie suckled a pebbled nipple through the cloth of the lightweight cami top. He made her wet and needy. Urged her to the edge. Made her wild. Being a fair sort, he switched to the other breast and she bucked, feeling his burgeoning arousal.

Her groan was louder than Archie's, and they both laughed.

"I want you so much it hurts." Her breathy admission made his eyes flare.

"Me too," he said.

They stripped off the rest of their garments and dove back onto the cushions together, falling in a tangle of limbs. Happiness a visible aura around them.

She had thought she wanted wild, but Archie's tender loving awed her. Teased her. Drove her off a precipice into a wondrous place of vibrant pleasure.

"What about you?" she murmured after her heartbeat slowed to normal.

"I am with you, sweetling." He stretched over her, slid between her thighs, and thrust. Her cry of joy was captured by a kiss. Their pace became frantic. In a quick move, he rolled them over without leaving her. "Ride me like you ride Dealanach Dubh."

Passion spiraling, she did. He panted, dug clenched fists into the cushions, cords bulged in his neck. Still she rode him hard. The coil within her tightened, snapped, and she tumbled over the precipice once again. His scream as his seed pulsed deep within her womb shook the glass windows.

Isobell dropped, limp, over Archie's chest, their hearts racing together, a secret smile on her lips. She would never forget this moment. When alone in this future place, she would hold the memory close to her heart. She blinked several times so not to shed a tear.

Archie covered them with his *plaide* and they cuddled for the longest time. "Isobell, I want you to come home with me. I ken that I cannot give you all these beautiful things." The wave of his arm encompassed the wee chamber, but she kenned the meaning—the luxury of this time. "But I will love you all of our days and nights."

"I dinnae want *things*. I want to go home with you, but I cannot."

"Why? Make me understand."

"Please. Just stay here with me." She used her eyes to sway him.

"Tell me why you believe you cannot come home with me." Archie thumped a finger against his chest.

"Because you will never forgive me."

"I already have."

"Nae. You dinnae understand." She sat up, clenching the *plaide* to her chest to cover her nudity. "You dinnae ken the extent of my activities with the reivers."

"Make me understand."

"I was the one who tended Maclay after his fall from the cliff and brought him back to health. I was the leader of the reivers." There she said it. She spoke the truth.

Archie's impassive stare made her feel clammy. Torturous moments passed. Finally, he pulled her into strong arms and tucked her head against his shoulder. "I am verra sorry you felt the need to hurt me."

What? "Why are you not yelling? Pushing me away?"

"You did what you believed you had to do—though it was based on lies. Because you thought I had done the same against your father and your clan."

"Aye."

"Your father has a lot to answer for."

"And you are willing to forgive me?"

"I already have." He pinned her with an intense look.

"You will give up your thieving ways."

"Those days are over." She glanced at her lap. "I cannot tell you who or where the reivers hide."

"Honor among thieves, aye?"

She raised her gaze to his. "Aye."

"You will come home with me."

The sweetest command she ever heard. "Aye." She felt his smile against her hair.

"You will need to make amends to those you wounded."

"How?"

"Perhaps through works of charity."

"I can do that." And she would. "I can help those who were hurt."

He pulled her down beside him and they snuggled close. "I love you with my heart, my soul, my life, forever."

"And I, you."

He kissed her, and everything within Isobell calmed. She was home in his arms.

Archibald shook her awake several hours later. "We have company, sweetling."

A grinning Munn stood over them with Caitrina at his back. The faerie held the gift box from Laurie. Munn carried her sword and Archie's claymore.

"You missed midnight services." Caitrina gave them a kenning smile. "It is time for you to return home."

The two fae creatures turned their backs so Isobell and Archie could dress with dignity. Isobell donned the gifted garments. Their family and new friends were waiting in the garden when they emerged from the orchid room.

After tearful goodbyes, Archibald clasped Isobell's hand. "Are you ready?"

"Aye."

A grave expression crossed his handsome face. "Forever?"

"Aye. Forever." She smiled, and his features softened.

Buoyed by a fated love, chief and lady-wife retreated from the garden, hand in hand, and walked just beyond the gate.

"I am scared," Isobell said, feeling the pull of the knoll.

CHAPTER THIRTEEN

*M*unn stepped toward the gate to follow Isobell and his chief. If he didn't hurry, he'd be left behind. His place was with the clan in the past.

Caitrina grabbed an arm and held him put. "They dinnae need you for their happily-ever-after."

"But—"

"This match is complete. A wee *bairn* will arrive in late September."

"Ach. I need to be there to protect the chief when he is called to war."

"We will ensure he sends others."

"Who can take his place?"

"Stephen will lead the chosen lads." Caitrina smiled. "We are off to other realms. 'Tis time to prepare for the next match."

"Tell me who the couple is." Munn glared at Caitrina. "I want to help with the final match of the queen's challenge."

The annoying faerie laughed. "I have decided to let you help. 'Tis Stephen and—"

"But you just said he will lead the lads."

"True."

Munn released a put out sigh. "With whom must he be

mated?"

"I had planned to tell you, but I have changed my mind. I will disclose the information when the time is right."

"Whatever."

"You have spent too much time in the future. You sound like the humans."

Munn shrugged. "A match for Stephen is impossible."

"Really?" Caitrina peered down her nose at him.

"Aye." Munn clenched his hands on his waist. "Stephen will be traveling far from Castle Lachlan and the *Sithichean Sluaigh*."

"Who claimed there is only one time gate?"

Archibald landed in a crouch on the green grass of the *Sithichean Sluaigh* as the sun's rays filtered through the trees onto the knoll. He took an unsteady breath. *Home.* He was definitely home. His favorite horse and Dealanach Dubh hoofed the snow just beyond the mound.

He tensed with panic. Where was Isobell? He spun around then released a relieved breath when she appeared at his side and stumbled into him.

"Dinnae ever want to do that again," she said as he righted her and she brushed dust from her *arisaid*.

Thank the good Lord. "Neither do I."

"Do you think 'twas naught but a dream?"

"'Twas real. We must keep this secret forever."

"Aye." She nodded earnestly. "Look. Dealanach Dubh."

She ran to the stallion and wrapped her arms around his neck. The sight warmed Archibald's heart.

"How do you think they came to be here?" Isobell asked when he joined her.

"I would imagine it has something to do with the fae." He shivered. He couldn't help it. The thought of fae magic still made him uneasy. "Shall we go home, sweetling?"

"Oh, aye." She frowned. "What will we tell the clan?"

"You were called away to care for your ailing aunt in

Glasgow where you had been living for the year before we wed. I went to fetch you."

"You think they will believe us?"

"They will not question their chief over such."

"What if one of the reivers is caught and accuses me of... You ken?"

Archibald gently squeezed her hand. "Nary a one will believe a thief over the wife of the clan chief."

She nodded. He lifted her onto Dealanach Dubh, leapt onto his mount, and they navigated the trail toward home. Cresting the final ridge, they took in the sight of Castle Lachlan.

"Beautiful," Isobell said, her voice laced with admiration. "Looks like one of those Christmas castles Mairi has on display at the inn."

"We must never mention seeing them."

"I ken." Her eyes misted. "I will miss them."

"As will I."

They rode to the stable where a signal was flashed to the castle. Holding hands, he and Isobell descended the slope to the beach. He helped her into a *currach*, joined her, and they were pulled over the partially frozen slush to the opposite shore where they were greeted by the *Lèine-chneas* and escorted into the castle.

In the great hall, servants scurried to and fro, readying the chamber for the holiday feast.

"Good Christmas morn," Aine greeted.

Archibald eased anxious muscles. 'Twas still Christmas. By the way Aine acted, they must not have been gone a lengthy time so it must still be the same year.

Isobell shivered, and Aine hustled them to the hearth where a large fire crackled.

"Great to see you, brother." Suibhne rose from one of the chairs. "May I return to university now?"

Archibald drew the young man into an awkward embrace, overjoyed to see him. The lad stiffened, never having been comfortable with familial affection. "You will stay for the feast and return to Glasgow tomorrow."

"As you wish." He inclined his head then smiled shyly at Isobell and bowed before dropping back into the chair and picking up the book he had been reading.

Suibhne had trained in fighting, yet preferred his studies. Frustrating. Archibald could use another strong arm with a calm head for the insecure times ahead. War with England was certainly on the horizon.

Dark thoughts for a bright day. Fortunately, Isobell's gentle fingers settling on his arm brought his attention to his lady-love.

"Shall we?" He escorted her to the head table where they partook of the holiday feast with the clan.

As the last course was served, the heavy oak door grated open, revealing Duncan and several other lads. Duncan strode to the dais to report. "Welcome back, my chief, my lady." He bowed.

"What have you to tell of Maclay and the reivers?" Archibald asked.

"We smoked them out of a hell-hole where they hid near the disputed lands. They won't be stealing anyone's cattle any more. Most of the reivers are dead."

"And Maclay?"

Duncan shook his head. "I am damned sorry. He escaped."

Would they never capture that bastard?

Isobell gripped his thigh, her nails digging into his skin through the wool of his *plaide*. He placed a hand over hers and leaned close. "Nae worries, sweetling. Maclay can't evade us forever and since we already ken of his rebirth, there is nae reason for the man to come after you."

She nodded then smiled at Duncan. "Please, sit. Enjoy your Christmas meal."

Archibald watched Duncan walk away then whispered so only Isobell could hear, "We will get through this. All will be well as long as we are together."

Her relieved smile melted his heart.

Later in their chamber, after making love, Archibald enjoyed the way she drew little circles on his bare arm. He felt more relaxed than he had since Patrick left. Maybe it was the kenning of what happened to his family. And the comfort of having his lady-wife with him...finally.

"I have something for you." He placed the ruby ring she'd left behind in her palm.

"Oh. Thank you." Her beautiful violet eyes misted then she frowned. "I left your ruby in the future with Patrick. I asked him to sell it for money to live on. I did not wish to be dependent on your family. With all that transpired after, I forgot to ask what happened to it."

"I have the ruby. He returned it to me."

"I am verra glad. It will be the envy of every warrior when it winks from your sword."

"And the target of every thief."

They both laughed.

"Would you like your other Christmas gifts?" Archibald asked.

"Later." With a sparkle in her eyes, she moistened her lips, and stole his breath with a kiss filled with promise.

They would be together. Forever.

Just Wait for Me

A Highland Gardens Novel
Book 3

Coming Soon
from
Dawn Marie Hamilton

www.dawnmariehamilton.com

Turn the page for a sneak peek…

PROLOGUE

9 September 1513 near the village of Branxton

*T*he king is dead.

Anguish tore from her halfling soul with a fae scream that reverberated over the field of devastation like rolling thunder.

Silence ensued. Men frozen in fear.

Caitrina dropped to her knees beside the redheaded warrior and ran gentle fingers along the bloodied curve of his handsome face. Damn Oonagh! Damn the fae queen! She'd refused to allow Caitrina to intervene in the politics of the mortals and prevent this tragedy.

Now, the king lay dead, fatally wounded by an arrow and a bill.

Be damned the English and their nasty weapon—the bill, a staff mounted with hooked chopping blade and pointed projections. The Scots hadn't stood a chance against the onslaught in this slippery, hilly terrain with their cumbersome pikes.

Heart broken, she cradled the man to her breast. Such greatness lost. Tears spilled unchecked onto his precious face. Too late. Even the magic tears of a *Sithichean* princess couldn't revive the king.

"Caitrina! Let us be away from here." The *brùnaidh*, the Maclachlan Clan brownie, fussed at her back. "We must remove Stephen from the field before the English learn he lives and plunge a bill into his chest."

She ignored the wee man. How would the Scots forge forward without their beloved king—with only a *bairn* and the sister of the despised English monarch to guide them?

"If we lose Stephen you will never regain your rightful place."

Aye. Oonagh and her stupid matchmaking challenge must be dealt with. Caitrina released James from her embrace and eased him to the ground. "Sleep in peace, oh greatest king."

The metallic tang of blood fouled the air. She rose and moved through the death and destruction. Oonagh had tricked her. Led her to believe after three matches she'd be free to return and live in *Tir-nan-óg*, the beloved faerie paradise, land o' heart's desire. But Oonagh had refused to reveal which match was the third and final. The one that would free Caitrina from servitude to the fae queen.

Caitrina and Munn had expended considerable energy on a third match. Only to learn Archibald and Isobell were the wrong couple. Therefore, one match remained to perform.

"Needs be we hurry!" Munn side-stepped one of the petrified English knights.

They found Stephen's prone form not far from that of his king. Caitrina rolled him over and took stock of his injuries. Thanks be to Danu, the blond warrior would live. She cloaked the three of them in fae mist and whisked them away on the fetid breeze to the healing caves of the Gray Women.

The battle field returned to morbid activity—an agony of pain.

CHAPTER ONE

Present Day, Greenbriar River Trail, West Virginia

"Rattlesnake!"

Jillian pedaled as fast as she could, past the autumn-tinted trees, to catch up to her brother, the rat. Why must he always speed ahead, leaving her in the dust?

"Kyle O'Donnell, did you hear me? I said...no, I screamed...rattlesnake."

As she rode the dusty mountain bike alongside, he slowed. "You overreact."

"Do not. There was a rattlesnake on the trail. What if the nasty snake bit me, and you were so far ahead you didn't know? The poison would be all through my system before help arrived."

Kyle chuckled. "That snake was more afraid of you than you of it. Relax."

She knew that, but wanted to make a point. "Why do you always dart ahead?"

"Because you're a slowpoke." He gave her a toothy grin. "I always wait for you to catch up. Don't I?"

Jillian gnashed her teeth. Why must he be so difficult? After all, Kyle was the one who had begged her to come on this stupid cycling trip. The least he could do was ride at her pace.

Who would have thought that at twenty-eight, and as a co-owner of a successful garden business, she still chased after her thirty-year-old sibling? She'd only agreed to join Kyle because she'd needed to get away. Away from all the happy-happy between Finn and Elspeth.

"Come on, the tunnel isn't far. Let's race." Her brother sped ahead again.

Jillian sighed and took her sweet time to catch up. Fifteen minutes later, she crossed the weathered old train trestle and arrived at the spot where Kyle waited, sporting an exasperated expression.

"Took you long enough."

Oh, how she wanted to kick him. Instead, she blew a kiss.

He brushed strands of annoyingly perfect sun-bleached, blond hair out of disgustingly gorgeous chocolate eyes and laughed. "Let's take a break before we ride through the tunnel."

So not fair. He got all the good looks and all their parent's attention. Geez. She was pathetic. Really. She needed to get over the past.

While they munched trail mix, Jillian covertly glanced into the rocky opening. The mouth of the abandoned train tunnel was dim and ominous. Water trickled from fissures in the stone walls and ceiling. A damp breeze wafting from the entrance brought with it a musty odor that drilled into her nostrils and sent a chill over her spine.

Did she want to ride through that murky place?

"Must we go through there? Couldn't we go back now and return to the last campsite? Enjoy the afternoon in the sun?"

"Don't you want to see what's on the other side?"

She stared into the dank tunnel. "Not really."

"Don't be a spoil sport. We haven't ridden enough miles today. I promise, after we go through the tunnel, we'll only ride another five. I heard there is a nice campground near a quaint town. Can you say restaurant?"

Jillian didn't want to go any farther, but knew there was

no use arguing. She'd never get Kyle to turn back. They would ride all the way to the southern end of the trail as planned.

She righted her bike and started walking toward the gloomy entrance. Clouds stole over the sun, making it difficult to see anything within. Jillian shivered. The hairs on her arms stood on end. Something didn't feel right about this place.

"Ready?" Kyle asked.

"No."

"Come on, Jilly. It'll be fun."

A couple on a silver tandem bicycle rode from the tunnel, waving as they passed. Sunshine reappeared from the clouds.

"See? It's safe," Kyle said.

"All right. But I'm going to walk my bike through. Just wait for me on the other side."

Kyle pedaled off, popped a wheelie, and entered the odious opening.

Jillian pulled a headlamp out of her pack, secured it over her baseball cap, and flicked it on. Inhaling deeply, she slowly walked her bike into the dark.

The beam of light bounced off brick walls and earthen floor. In the far distance, hazy sunlight indicated the other end of the tunnel. Okay, she could do this. There was nothing here to fear. She proceeded carefully, taking shallow breaths. About a quarter of the way through, rough rock replaced brick on the walls. A blast of super-cold air hit her side.

She shined the light into what appeared to be a passageway. Narrow and foreboding. Suddenly, something pressed against her back. A hand? Her pulse quickened. Whoa! A dizzy sensation swamped her senses. She stumbled. Lost hold of the bike. Fell—or was she being pulled?

She tumbled into the mysterious opening. Falling downward, her body became weightless as she plummeted down...down...down...into a black void. Colorful lights erupted in her mind. A horrible buzzing assaulted her ears.

She screamed, but no sound passed her parched lips.

A piercing white light appeared, drawing her to it. She closed her eyes, but felt no relief. Pain burst behind heavy lids, making her head throb relentlessly. Bile burned her throat. Just when the agony became too much to endure, the cruel light exploded into a zillion pieces.

Blue stars twinkled in a peaceful midnight sky. Her mind blanked.

Panting, Jillian crouched, tips of fingers pressed against the earth for balance. The nauseous sensation gradually subsided and she attempted to stand. Vertigo forced her to her knees, and her stomach lurched again.

Breathe, Jillian. Breathe.

She inhaled deep breaths, trying to calm down. The nausea finally passed and she sat against the rough trunk of a tree. Exhaustion tempted her to curl up and sleep. But she needed to hurry and catch up with…Kyle.

Where was he? Where was she?

Jillian didn't recognize the surroundings. The towering evergreens were larger than any she'd ever seen before, heavy needles blocking a majority of the late afternoon light. The dense forest wasn't like any they'd cycled through on this trip.

She started to shake. This was no time to come unglued. She inhaled a deep, calming breath. Think, Jillian, analyze the situation. *How did you get here?* Her last memory was entering the train tunnel and falling. Had someone shoved her? She'd thought she felt the pressure of a hand on her back as she'd fallen forward.

Strange. Who would have pushed her? No one came to mind. They'd only seen the couple on the tandem, riding the other way. No other cyclists or hikers.

Frowning, she removed one of the water bottles attached to her pack, took a long swig, and accessed the height of the sun. There wasn't much time before it would get dark. She scanned the area. Great. Her bike was missing and there was no sign of a trail.

Nerves taut, she swallowed hard. She would not submit to

fear. If she started walking, surely she'd come across a road or some such thing. *Right?*

Jillian walked until she couldn't take another step. Her feet hurt. Sneakers were little protection against the rough, rocky terrain. The sun was setting, and she was lost. Completely and utterly lost, but she refused to panic. She would find a safe place to settle in for the night. Tomorrow she was sure to find some sign of civilization.

On a scree covered slope, she spotted a protected area under an overhanging ledge. She scrambled up the incline, slipping and sliding, scraping knees and hands. She had fleece cover-ups, a wind jacket, and a space blanket in her pack. Pulling out the silver cloth, she laid it on the ground. She slipped into the fleece and zipped the jacket snug as the sun disappeared over the horizon.

Wanting to save the batteries in the headlamp, she ate a power bar in the dark. She wrapped the blanket around her, and used the pack as a pillow. She hummed. When that didn't ease the jitters, she made up silly stories as a distraction. Small stones dug into her side, but finally, exhaustion took hold and she slept.

Thunder from a passing storm woke her at some point. The feeling someone watched skittered over her nerves. She blinked, trying to adjust her vision to the dark. Nighttime forest sounds heightened her anxiety. She expected to see glowing animal eyes. But no, as far as she could tell, she was alone.

Nervous and stiff, it took a while to fall asleep again only to startle awake before dawn. The storm had passed and a bright silver moon slid in and out of clouds, creating shifting shadows. An odd disfiguration of bark at the bottom of a nearby tree caught Jillian's attention. The scarred wood appeared as a young boy's face.

Staring hard at the tree, she smiled as the face changed in the moon's unpredictable light. Two distinctly different faces appeared imbedded in the rough bark. The first, a boy with a pudgy nose and big sad eyes, and the second—

She must be dehydrated. Delusional. Imagining faces imbedded in a perfectly normal tree. Jillian huddled deeper into the cocoon the space blanket provided and tried to fall back to sleep.

Sleep wouldn't come so she glanced at the tree again. A third face appeared in the texture of the old oak. This one had a scarred forehead and a crooked mouth.

Such fanciful thoughts. She snorted. Here she was lost and alone in the woods and she was killing time imagining faces in a tree trunk. Sleep was what she needed. In her mind, she counted plants on a potting bench in the greenhouse at *Foxgloves*—one hundred thirty two, thirty three, thirty four.

Finally, Jillian dozed off again.

When she woke a third time, a chill had seeped into her bones. She sat up and pulled the space blanket more snuggly around her. The tree looked different in the white light of morning and another image appeared. This tiny face had an elongated nose and wisps of blond hair dangled across its brow. Jillian covered her mouth to stifle a giggle. She'd recently read a book about faeries and changelings and stolen children. She imagined that the hobgoblins lived in this tree. That stolen boys—

The snap of a branch made her jump. Her stomach knotted.

Standing before her was a gnarled little man. No more than four feet tall, he nearly blended into the surrounding woods. The peculiar clothes he wore matched the colors of the forest. And his dusty brown skin had wrinkles upon wrinkles. Elf-like ears stuck out from beneath a pointed cap. But what startled her most, were the unusual blue-green eyes that bore into her.

The man reminded her of a sketch she'd seen while babysitting. Little Allison MacLachlan loved the story of *Rumpelstiltskin*.

Jillian clutched the space blanket in fists and gawked at the man. He stared back. Unnerving seconds passed in silence. Abruptly, the strange fellow lunged forward and yanked on the blanket, almost snatching it away.

"What do you think you're doing? Leave my blanket alone." She rose into a crouch, holding tight to the silver cloth while he continued to tug. When the man let go, Jillian fell backward unto her rump. "Dammit."

His eyes narrowed. "Be you a witch?"

"What?" She shook her head. "Of course not."

He circled around. "Then who are you to have spun such a plaid. You are nae one of the *Sithichean*. Are you?"

Her thoughts whirled. "A what?"

"A *Sithichean*, one of the faeries of these hills." A wave of an arm encompassed the surrounding terrain.

Jillian ran fingers along the edge of the space blanket. "This isn't a plaid."

The man glowered.

Ridiculous. "Who are you?"

"That is none of your mind. My lad be needing that plaid." He grabbed for the blanket again.

She drew it close to her chest, refusing to let go. Jillian wasn't about to let the crazy little man steal it. "I asked who you are."

He raised his chin defiantly. "You tell me first."

"Oh, all right. I'm tired of this game." Jillian threw up her arms in exasperation. "I'm Jillian O'Donnell. I'm lost. Perhaps you can direct me to the nearest road?"

A mischievous glint flashed in the man's eyes. "There are none, but if you give me that plaid, I'll tell you where to find a game trail."

"Will that take me into town?"

"None here or about. Nearest village is three days walk over yonder ridge." He pointed off to the left.

While she glanced that way, the man snatched the blanket and disappeared into the wood.

Hands fisted on hips Jillian glared at the trees. "Damned little man."

There wasn't a spot on Stephen's black and blue body that didn't hurt. The battle had been a bloodbath. Although his wounds weren't too serious, he ached everywhere.

And his leg—would be awhile before it healed.

His memory burned with the haunting sight of his dead monarch. Stephen had never expected events to unfold as they had. King James the IV of Scotland, dead on the battlefield beside so many of the kingdom's finest warriors.

After lying unconscious among the dead, Stephen had managed to escape the chaos of the field with the help of Munn, the MacLachlan Clan brounie, and found shelter in the caves of the Gray Women. Stephen didn't remember how they'd managed the feat, but here he was, hidden away from those who'd wish him ill.

Stifling a groan, he shifted the bum leg and reached for what Munn procured. His fingers slid over an unusual, shiny fabric. "What the devil? Where did you get this bewitched cloth?"

Munn looked away, and an uncomfortable dread ran through Stephen. The brownie scraped a foot in the dirt. Stephen's teeth chattered so he wrapped the strange cloth around his upper body. Whether from witch or fae, he was cold and needed any warmth the strange fabric could provide.

"Munn? Where did you get it?"

"Forest."

"Who did you steal it from?"

"Borrowed." Blue-green eyes flashed. "There be a lass in the wood. Dressed as a lad."

"What were you thinking, wee man? We don't want to be discovered." Stephen swallowed uneasily. "Is the wench English?"

Munn curled his body away and looked over his shoulder at Stephen as if bracing for a blow. "Foreign. Like Lady Laurie."

Stephen inhaled sharply. *Like Lady Laurie?* Was it possible? "Fetch her here."

"'Twould be a mistake."

"Do as I say. But be careful. We dinnae want the English to find us."

With a deep grumble, Munn scurried out of the cave.

Stephen scrubbed the stubble on his chin. Could another time traveler have appeared at the *Sithichean Sluaigh*, the faerie mound near Castle Lachlan? If so, how would she have gotten here? 'Twas quite a distance from Strathlachlan.

Hmmm. Would the lass be as intriguing as Lady Laurie?

Just Beyond the Garden Gate
Book One, Highland Gardens Series

by Dawn Marie Hamilton

Time Travel Fantasy Romance

Determined to regain her royal status, a banished faerie princess accepts a challenge from the High-Queen of the Fae to unite an unlikely couple while the clan brownie attempts to thwart her.

Passion ignites when a faerie-shove propels burned-out business consultant Laurie Bernard through the garden gate, back through time, and into the embrace of Patrick MacLachlan. The arrogant clan chief doesn't know what to make of the lass in his arms, especially when he recognizes the brooch she wears as the one his stepmother wore when she and his father disappeared.

With the fae interfering at every opportunity, the couple must learn to trust one another while they battle an enemy clan, expose a traitor within their midst and discover the true fate of the missing parents. Can they learn the most important truth—love transcends time?

Journey from the lush gardens of the Blue Ridge Mountains of North Carolina to the Scottish Highlands of 1509 with *Just Beyond the Garden Gate*.

Just Once in a Verra Blue Moon
Book Two, Highland Gardens Series

by Dawn Marie Hamilton

Time Travel Fantasy Romance

What happens when a twenty-first century business executive is expected to fulfill a prophecy given at the birth of a sixteenth-century seer? Of course, he must raise his sword in her defense.

Believing women only want him for his wealth, Finn MacIntyre doesn't trust any woman to love him. When, during Scottish Highland games, faerie magic sends him back in time to avenge the brutal abduction of his time-traveling cousin, he learns he's the subject of a fae prophecy.

Elspeth MacLachlan, the beloved clan seer, is betrothed to a man she dislikes and dreams of the man prophesized at her birth, only to find him in the most unexpected place— facedown in the mud.

With the help of fae allies, they must overcome the treachery set to destroy them to claim a love that transcends time.

Journey from the lush gardens of the Blue Ridge Mountains of North Carolina to the Scottish Highlands of 1511 with *Just Once in a Verra Blue Moon*.

Sea Panther
Book One, Crimson Storm Series

by Dawn Marie Hamilton

Paranormal Romance

2013 Golden Heart® finalist for Best Paranormal Romance

Can love mend a fractured soul?

After evading arrest for Jacobite activities, Scottish nobleman Robert MacLachlan turns privateer. A Caribbean Voodoo priestess curses him to an eternal existence as a vampire shifter torn between the dual natures of a Florida panther and an immortal blood-thirsting man. For centuries, he seeks to reverse the black magic whilst maintaining his honor. Cruising the twenty-first century Atlantic, he becomes shorthanded to sail his 90-foot yacht, *Sea Panther*. The last thing he wants is a female crewmember and the call of her blood.

Although she swore never to sail again after her father died in a sailing accident, Kimberly Scot answers the captain's crew wanted ad to escape a hit man. She's lost everything, her fiancé, her job, and most of her money, along with money belonging to her ex-clients. A taste of Kimberly's blood convinces Robert she is the one woman who can claim the panther's heart. To break the curse, they travel back in time to where it all began—Jamaica 1715.

Future Works:

Time Travel Fantasy Romance

Just Wait for Me
Book Three, Highland Gardens Series

Paranormal Romance

Raven's Revenge
Book Two, Crimson Storm Series

ABOUT THE AUTHOR

Dawn Marie Hamilton dares you to dream. She is a 2013 RWA® Golden Heart® Finalist who pens Scottish-inspired fantasy and paranormal romance. Some of her tales are rife with mischief-making faeries, brownies, and other fae creatures. More tormented souls—shape shifters, vampires, and maybe a zombie or two—stalk across the pages of other stories. She is a member of The Golden Network, Fantasy, Futuristic & Paranormal, Celtic Hearts, and From the Heart chapters of RWA. When not writing, she's cooking, gardening, or paddling the local creeks of Southern Maryland with her husband.

Visit Dawn Marie on the web at dawnmariehamilton.com.

www.ingramcontent.com/pod-product-compliance
Lightning Source LLC
Chambersburg PA
CBHW030543130626
46552CB00006B/2401